Blood, etc

Award-winning poet and dramatist Gee Williams was born in Flintshire. *Blood, etc* is her second collection of short fiction.

Blood, etc

Gee Williams

PARTHIAN

Parthian
The Old Surgery
Napier Street
Cardigan
SA43 1ED

www.parthianbooks.co.uk

First published in 2008
© Gee Williams 2008
All Rights Reserved

ISBN 978-1-905762-07-1

Editor: Gwen Davies

Cover design & photography by Lucy Llewellyn
Inner design by books@lloydrobson.com
Printed and bound by Gomer Press, Llandysul,
Wales

Published with the financial support of the Welsh
Books Council.

British Library Cataloguing in Publication Data

A cataloguing record for this book is available from
the British Library.

for David

and in memory of William Allen Jones
(whoever you were)

Contents

Blood, etc

The house, Carousel – a piss-poor, schmaltzy, inappropriate name for a buff-brick nineteen-thirties house, he thought – stood at a bit of a crossroads. Not a roundabout, which might at least have made explicable the overlarge sign they were always meaning to get changed. Just a crossroads. A crossing of two unimportant minor roads, neither of which provided the best or shortest route to the built-up areas they joined together. Tatten Lane passed under Carousel's front wall. It brought sporadic traffic to annoy anyone attempting to read in the sitting room or sleep in the guest bedroom, before it wandered off in the direction of the river and the old pack-horse bridge. Only an ugly bungalow (dwarfed by stables the size and shape of a modern factory unit) stood between Carousel and where Dial Green petered out. The wider Old Wrexham Road ran along the side of the house. It made for the country town with more obvious brio but was kept at bay by a large, shrubby garden and the remains of an ancient orchard. In season its ripe fruit, spurned by the inhabitants of Carousel, still fell from the branches, rolled onto the tarmac and were pulped by passing cars...

Or were snatched up by the more quick-witted of the animals being chivvied to and from Tatten Livery by a succession of lithe, young riders. All female.

When they moved in Mel must've been one of the first locals he'd become aware of: a young girl – that's the mistake he'd made and only when already close enough for speech had Alun clocked how, under the hat – the *helmet* – there was a girl/woman.

Round, fresh face. Dark, slightly protuberant eyes under fleshy lids. Freckles across the nose and upper cheekbones. When she smiled it was with rows of small regular teeth, though a shade too ivory for perfection. When she swept off the hat, whose black silk cover had slipped askew giving her a bit of a tipsy air, the red hair sprang shocking out.

Sixteen he reckoned. (Afterwards, after the accident and the passing around of fragments of that day's happening as though they were a new currency the whole neighbourhood had gone over to, he'd found she was nearer twenty.)

'Let him have it!' he'd suggested as he saw the huge horse snatch at the bit, lunge forward in its quest for fruit and the rider with equal determination haul on the reins. 'Let him have an apple. They're only going to waste.'

'That's not the point!' Mel had snapped back.

'Isn't it?'

The horse swung immense, brown hindquarters at Alun's face and he dodged back to the sanctuary of steps up to his gate. A spark was kindled as the iron shoe struck a stone where an instant ago his own feet had stood. He'd never seen that before, but then he'd not had much to do with horses before. 'Why isn't it?'

Breathing hard with the effort the girl circled the horse and its threatening hooves out into the lane before turning its head in Alun's direction as though the animal were a boat in a heavy swell and Alun waiting on the dockside. 'Because,' she said, still panting, 'he mustn't think – stand up, Samson, stand up! – he mustn't think when he's working he can just stop for something to eat. When he wants. He has to–' but in giving her attention to Alun for the moment it took to frame the reply, Samson had shot out his muzzle and grabbed up a half-apple from the gutter. The blunt lower jaw slid from side to side as the fruit was pulverised and the juice ran. And there was nothing Mel could do to hinder it.

'Seems to me,' said Alun, 'that's exactly what he can do.'

Mel had let out a hoot of laughter and slapped the blissfully masticating brute on its arched neck. 'I know! He's a greedy sod. Just look at the weight on him.'

It gave him a thrill that voice. Not because it was anything special. Not because of its light, girly tone and easy half-Welsh, half-English border accent. But because it was not the voice of a three-year-old boy – the only other, apart from his own, he heard all day. Not that looking after the child, his child, was bad – how could he ever allow himself to think that? Or if it was, when it was, it couldn't be blamed on Charlie. That day, the day he'd first spoken to Mel, he'd retraced his steps and picked the boy from the lawn and hoisting him onto his shoulders had said, 'Come and see the big horse, Charlie,' and Charlie had shrieked with excitement at the movement and new elevation.

'Hor-orse! Hor-orse!' the child demanded.

'D'you want a ride Charlie, hey? A ride on the horse? Can he?' he added almost as a formality and in the act of passing the small body from his own shoulders to the animal's neck.

Samson's head jerked towards his massive chest as he reined back one stride, two strides, out of reach. 'No, sorry,' Mel said. The action had seemed like a rejection from the horse itself but now he realised it was just a trick, a manoeuvre inspired by some signal of hand and heel that he'd missed. 'Too dangerous. The kid could get hurt.' She sent further directions to the beast – ah, yes, he saw that one: the left boot tap, the right rein twitched – and away they went leaving him standing, the child still offered up in his arms.

The kid? Alun's temper kindled at the slight. *The kid?* Immersed for the better part of Charlie's short life in Charlie's care, his desire to indulge the boy was affectively maternal though masculine in sheer force. His own belief in Charlie's status as a small but priceless household god was rarely subject to challenge.

'Miserable bitch,' he muttered.

But she was right. Imagine the possibilities, the explanations and Holly's face, angry, flushed and incredulous. *You did what? And then what? Christ Alun, what the fuck were you thinking of?*

What the fuck had he been thinking of? Of course she was right.

And a good thing not to have taken against Mel, newcomer as he was. No one the length of the straggling, half-pretty place had a word to say against Mel and he soon learned why. She and Samson were local celebrities. Twice daily they'd make their way though the alarums and excursions of The

4

Square to gain access to the old bridleway running over the hill, mile after mile. Local lads – rough as they looked – raised unironic open bottles to them as they passed in front of The Pendy Arms or The Full Moon. *Mel and Samson had once been on television.* You don't go disrespecting someone who's been interviewed for nearly a minute on *Wales Today*. And Mel acknowledged them. Though she came from The Old Rectory, though her father was a consultant at Maelor Ears, Nose and Throat – and wealthy enough to keep a jobless daughter and a vast, money-munching horse – Mel acknowledged them. (*Hi-yer, Scott! See you, then, Tim!* The first time Alun witnessed it, he found himself troubled with unaccountable pain). She nodded to Scott and Tim and the weaselly Neil. She nodded to the driver of the ad-daubed single-decker bus that backed up onto the garage forecourt rather than crowd Dial Green's star. In the store, Mel and Samson's success at the last Royal Welsh Show remained prominent, if yellowing, in the window. The horse's bulk improbably hovered over a construction of striped poles and Mel's small figure, well out of the saddle, hovered above him. Gravity, the picture demonstrated, gravity – for those with the knack – was a sometime force.

On local radio one endless afternoon 'a young Dial Green rider proves unbeatable' was actually the before-these-and-other-stories headline. Or it was until an explosion at the soap-powder plant knocked it out of its slot.

One endless afternoon...

In the city where he and Holly'd met, in the tight, modern flat they'd brought Charlie home to, the afternoons hadn't had so many hours in them. It was something to do with the view, he decided. In the city you were connected to a squirming vista, opening up and closed down by high-sided traffic so that

5

pass the window on your way to the kitchen and a whole Victorian canyon of buildings terminated only in the distant prospect of the Cathedral – look again on your return trip and the Japanese tourists in a coach not ten feet away smiled up at you, edgily courteous. Beyond your window, in any half-day period (the time between Holly popping in to breastfeed Charlie his lunch, say, and the first hope of her return) – beyond your window was bound to offer something in the way of a buzz. A rear-ending with or without rage, an assisted fall from a bike... a dog's suicidal dash into the carriage-way, lead flapping. He had enjoyed a bag-snatch, a police-car's totalling against a concrete bollard and an old lady's collapse and removal by paramedics without accompanying siren – so a probable death right there as he watched.

'How awful!' Holly had murmured over her pasta.

A jolt. Yes, it was awful, wasn't it, another human being subsiding beneath you, breathing her last next to the teak-effect structure holding communal bins?

In Dial Green there was no movie running constantly within the window frame. No free, chaotic fringe-show. There was a painting. The trees in the redundant orchard made him cranky with their sluggard ways. 'When are we going to see some apples on those things?'

'Don't be impatient – the blossom's only just fallen.'

Holly was country-bred as Charlie was going to be. Holly had been accurate in this as in most else. Apples had appeared in pointless, messy profusion – and he'd spoken to Mel.

Was it the height of the horse that meant she always had him at a disadvantage? It was a couple of weeks later. The boy was having a nap and Alun was released into the September sunshine and free from the nagging vigilance of care. Mel had surprised him on his own property. He was caught examining fruit still attached to a squat, cankerous branch of apple that was becoming lost in an unpruned briar.

'I'll bet you've got enough there for a ton of jam.'

He spun round to see her head and shoulders above the hedge. Slowly, weirdly, the disembodied living bust slid along the shaggy hedge-top, turned and slid back to its original position but facing the other way.

'*Jam?*'

The fruit already picked that was in his free hand he dropped to the grass.

'Well if it was me, I'd do cider. I think the old bid lived here before you did cider. Always had a smile on her face.'

He shrugged. Beyond the hawthorn the horse snorted and a V-sign of brown ears flicked up.

He could play the townie: 'All this – it needs cutting back. I thought – probably get someone in to do it. Someone who knows what they're doing. Not my thing – all this.'

It was the truth – the near truth. That morning Holly had suggested he harvest and stew fruit for Charlie's tea. ('They must be organic, right? I mean we've been here since the spring. Nobody's sprayed them.') Patiently, whilst fending off his help to zip up the grey dress, shaking out the black jacket, matador-style, she'd explained. How you just peeled a good big apple, cut it up, cooked it in a pan, stirred in that Manuka honey she's just managed to get hold of that was going to be good for Charlie's gripy tummy. How it wasn't rocket-science for Chrissake.

But what was a good apple? Not bruised... not already home to a tetchy wasp. Even on the tree every fruit he examined had some sort of mark or excavation. Did this mean it was not good?

'So what is your thing then?'

'Well – what do I do, d'you mean?'

'If you like.'

'I'm on a break at the moment.'

'Sick leave is it?' It was said, he felt, with a challenge in the tone even though it hadn't made it onto the face.

Cow! He really didn't want to get into this. But where was the refuge from the smiling down, provocative child – yes, child he still thought her. This must be innocence rather than goading – surely? A misreading. Of something not meant or not understood. Not yet experienced. In your thirties you were about as far away from teenagers as you were going to get: twice their years, off the pace of their culture but still with only babies and toddlers amongst your friends and in your own house – so no new perspective there either....

'A career break. We've got the little fellow in there.' *Bollocksfuckingbollocks*. 'We-er had the kid, you know and one of us had to take a break. Holly, that's my partner, she helps run a business. It's a leather factor, if you know what that is. They deal in all types of leather. It's in the city – in Chester. She runs it really. So it was easier for me to... just till we get him off to school. It's good. It's been good. I...'

'Yeah? See you.'

The truck that was suddenly there beside him on the Wrexham Road, its air-brakes hissing, was a sort of comfort. It drove off Samson with his inquisitive passenger and allowed Alun to get inside, though appleless... Charlie, must check on Charlie.

Up in the small bed with its racing-car modelling, the

boy slept on, one finger hooked into his light brown curls. He knelt beside him and gently pulled down the child's hand and, though gummed with chocolate, tucked it beneath the quilt – for what reason? Did he want to wake him? No, of course not and yes, he needed to have Charlie awake so that he could make amends in play or treats. He needed to make up to Charlie for the disquiet that had come over him out there in the orchard, being questioned by that brainless girl. *Sick leave!* But the boy, though he stirred, burrowed down again into sleep. Against the weight of the covering, the sticky fingers flapped uselessly and stilled. He ought to wake him – tonight as they attempted to eat off their separate trays Charlie, alert and demanding would give the game away. Cantering laps of the room, pretending to show-jump Holly's outstretched legs and failing – and delighting in the failure with thought-numbing screams.

How long did you leave this child down?

That afternoon he found a machete-type thing in one of the locked outhouses they had yet to clear out. With the boy still sleeping soundly he took it to the briars in the hedge and several other overgrown bushes he couldn't identify; he hacked and decapitated with wired intensity. *Sick leave.* As though hawking around cheap (slash) fucking rancid (slash) hides was such a big deal. As though minding (slash) your own child (slash) was so (slash) fuckingoffthefuckingwall. As though sticking manfully to the cause of Durward (slash) Leather Ltd was going to find the cure for cancer.

'And is it all chugging along as normal at Skin City?' he asked Holly almost before she'd put down her keys and looked around for Charlie, 'He's that heap of sand, by the way, driving the fire-engine.'

'Oh, well done Alun!' Holly was out of the back door, picking her way down the uneven path in black five-inch heels. 'Hello yuk-mush!' She picked the giggling Charlie up and carried him in at arm's length. 'You could get him cleaned up when you know I'm coming home. What time is it? It's gone seven for FS.'

'You like to bath him on a Friday. You said...'

'I know. *I know*. But you could have given him a lick and a promise first.'

'I'll do it now. Just give him to me.'

'Doesn't matt...'

The pair disappeared up the stairs. Ten minutes later, changed, different, all smiles, they were back... Charlie standing on the rug between them, his unclouded blue eyes fixed on Holly's face – *as they did the instant the very instant the exact instant she came into a room*.

'Early frost, eh?' This from the student working out the summer's end at the garage, behind armoured glass. Alun had spoken to him a couple of times, knew more than he needed to know, now, about his parents' giving up the farm, his course in Forestry at Bangor, his debts. No name.

'Is it?'

'Well – yeah. Don't usually get it white over, not October, do we?'

He pocketed the card – 'To be honest, I haven't a clue' – never for a second taking his attention from the VW out on the forecourt, from Charlie, trapped in his seat, staring good-naturedly about him.

An October frost – that was meant to mean something was it? Put on the spot, he realised, he couldn't have told the exact date and would've had to grope for the month. As he sat, feet up on the kitchen table and the Driving section of last Sunday's paper open before him, he made a point of noting *October 10, 2004*. So – today was the 12th... a date completely without significance of any sort. It wasn't a day away from that important decision on his productivity bonus. No new and fragile contact at The Club Chair Company needed to be inveigled out to lunch. And as for that flight to Stuttgart the lame-brain Julie had forgotten to book, it had turned out to be no bad thing because that had been the week World of Bags had come back to him with the biggest, single...

Swinging down numbed legs he was straight up onto his feet. The paper slipped into its constituent pages onto the floor and he crumpled it for the recyc rather than bother with reassembly. How pathetically easy it was for the brain to stumble into this sort of thing! Present events, hateful as they unfold but their edges gradually smoothed over by memory to become cosy, funny: to become *Well, of course, at the time, while you're doing it, it can be an absolute nightmare but you get a real rush when you pull off a...*

An early frost, was it? OK. A spur to replacing those broken flags before the weather worsened, before Holly in her beautiful brush-dyed, scarlet leather knee-highs went arse over tit. Charlie was uncomplaining as, re-buttoned into a jacket, he was piggy-backed outside. 'Right, Charles William Mann, your mission, should you chose to accept it, is to lever up these broken bits, stack them out of sight behind the outhouse because Daddy has no idea what you're meant to do with spare bits of path and then bring those four new slabs that have been sitting round the front for over a month and drop then neatly into place. They will of course be a perfect fit.'

11

Charlie, nodding, made a move to pick up the crowbar (another outhouse find) but when Alun said, 'No! That's for Daddy to use,' a cynical look crossed his three-year-old face. He trotted off in the direction of the swing singing 'Per-erflect fit, per-erflect fit' in his clear treble. 'Don't worry there'll be something for you in a minute...' Alun couldn't think what though. 'And then you can help me with the really hard part, yeah?' The child didn't even favour this one with a backward glance. The path was history. Down the garden, that's where it was happening... determination to be there was written into his spine, in his arms swinging, despite the padded coat. But small for his age: the observation came accompanied by a slight niggle, a psychic pin-prick. Was Charlie destined to be not only light-boned and pale as Holly but also more Holly-beneath-the-skin? Attention easily focused and biddable as a tuning button, cutting from this to that message, the fuzzy to the sharp. Nothing ever got to Holly, as they said at the Chester office, because Holly *didn't let it*.

The stack of four flags – no five flags, one for breakages, of course – was nestling in its fringe of long grass behind the front hedge. Misjudging size Alun rammed them with the wheelbarrow – and did it again. He could at least have offered Charlie a ride around in the barrow, something that never failed to delight. When he'd got this first one shifted, he'd do it for the next and the next. He bent to the task.

From beyond the hedge, there were three distinct sounds. (Later he'd be able to work out that these were the incident itself and everything else its aftermath). First came a female voice: a shout that began as 'Whoah-h!' but carried on beyond the word as 'oh-oh-oh!' until drowned out by the second noise, an easily identifiable squeal of brakes. This ended in a thud, dull but with metallic overtones. There were a few seconds of silence during which Alun let go the slab almost trapping his own fingers and stood up. Just over the hedge, but very close to it, was the silver roof of an estate car. He had a moment to recognise it (he was good on cars) as a Mercedes when a new sound started up. It was the worst thing he had heard in his life: a deep, throaty bellow that rose and slackened, rocketed up to an almost unbearable pitch before subsiding into a thick gurgle. Another bellow – more gurgling – a blessed pause – and a horrible human-like scream.

The steps down onto the road were almost blocked by the car's bonnet but he fought the hawthorn to get out. Hidden by the car but now directly ahead of him he came across Mel. She was lying on her side, one arm beneath her head, which was turned toward him. Her eyes were wide open and apparently staring into his. Her hat was still in place though pushed back so that strands of bright red hair were on show and there was a long black mark across her cheek. As he knelt down to touch her face and speak a word to her, the off-side door of the Mercedes (with its dented panel) began to swing open. It would, he saw, catch the unmoving Mel in its arc. Angrily he placed both fists on the door and slammed it shut. A face behind the glass – with an open mouth – registered with him as nobody, neither man nor woman.

'Stay in!' he shouted at it. Dimly he was aware that in the vehicle's interior someone had begun to cry.

Mel blinked.

'It's all right but you shouldn't move,' he said to her. He patted the arm that lay along the road surface – in fact, had become a part of the road's surface. The green material of her sleeve was ripped away and her lower arm embedded with gravel. A terrible mewling rose again from somewhere beyond them and Mel screwed up her eyes as though wishing someone, somewhere would just turn it down. She groaned and flopped over onto her back. 'Oh fuck,' she breathed but managed to straighten out her legs.

'You really have got to keep still...'

'Sam-son.'

'What?'

Her hand, its palm dark with grit and blood gestured to somewhere else, somewhere vaguely in the direction of town. 'The fucking horse!' she shouted furiously.

'But...'

'I'm all... right. *Listen*! Go!'

It didn't occur to him to do anything but follow such fierce instructions. Certainly not to turn back to the car and its occupants. Around the corner he found the animal, half of it lying across the grass verge, the rest (the brown heap of its hindquarters and a pair of threshing back legs) sticking out into Wrexham Road. Across the way a motorcyclist had dismounted but stood, visor down, his back to his machine, not moving. Ahead a white van was pulled up on the opposite verge and its driver just getting out. 'D'you have a mobile?' he had to shout above the horse's terrific bellows which had grown at his approach. The man nodded and fumbled at his belt unable to look away from the animal on the ground. 'Call the police and ambulance and – and a vet. Say people hurt – and a horse. Badly injured. OK? Yes? Corner of Old Wrexham Road and Tatten Lane. Yes?' In a wide curve he walked to the front of Samson. To the approaching van-driver he said. 'Can you go into the lane and check on the girl – the rider – and whoever's in that fucking car? Can you, please?' Just as he

14

had felt impelled to do with Mel, he knelt down and patted what was closest – in this case a thick, twitching foreleg with its white sock. Samson rolled his eyes and screamed and a violent shudder travelled along his body. Two iron shoes clattered on the tarmac. Alun pulled his hand away. He could see now the explanation of the creature's complaint. The upper right foreleg and right shoulder were not so much injured as mashed: there was a reduction to a bloody ragout of tissue where a robust, load-bearing joint had once been. What had become of the hide in this area with its cover of brown hair was a mystery. No sign of it. It was as though this had been completely dissolved in the impact: the guard was off the machine and the works were on show. Creamy subcutaneous fat and the humps of muscle, grey wires connecting this with that, white and pearly-pink shards of bone, all had come spilling out. Incredible that such a blunt-instrument as a car had done this... easier to believe in a shot-gun, a bomb-blast, a mauling by lions.

The waxing and waning of distress was the result of the animal's attempt to rise. With stupid persistence, Samson drew his hind legs under him and tried to heave himself up to a comical sitting position. The left foreleg straightened but wasn't anywhere near up to the job of raising such a weight alone. Repeatedly he slumped back onto the turf as blood and gobbets from the gaping hole in his right side sprayed out. Alun thought of catching at the broken rein that hung from the bit, wondering if he had the strength to hold the suffering horse down. Never having so much as touched Samson in the weeks of their acquaintance (having been threatened, in fact, by his wayward nature and size) dare he take charge of the animal now, in its last few minutes of life?

Suddenly Mel was beside him. The flayed arm hung by her side and either she or someone else had taken off her hat.

'Christ, you shouldn't be up.'

Her face was the colour of plaster and seemed to set as she looked down. 'I'm all right – just my wrist. Can you help me get this jacket off?'

'Why don't you wait for the ambulance? Let them decide...'

Already she had the good arm free. 'Are you going to help or what?'

Gently as he could, Alun pulled the stiff garment off her. She dropped onto the grass, not able to kneel, and took hold of the bridle. Surely she lacked the strength to hold the head in place? And yet from her touch, beginning in her fingers, some new force flowed. Though the leather of noseband and cheek-pieces it shot, through the half-dead-half-living fabric of the straps and into the horse's jagged nerves. It was as though the animal paused, just for an instant, in its simple program of flight: Mel let go the rein and carefully placed part of the olive stuff of her jacket across Samson's eyes. The long rasping in his throat continued and he began to grind his teeth, horribly – Alun felt he must be sheering off the enamel with the force of it – but the great legs stilled.

'Is that what you're meant to do? To keep them quiet?'

'I don't know – how the fuck do I know? It's just something I've seen on the TV.'

Apart from the slowing of the occasional car – to be waved away by Alun – a sort of peace descended on the three of them. Mel sat bare-armed, pale but not crying, not shivering or moving much at all, one usable hand on the horse's forehead and its blindfold. Her arms, he saw, were

16

nothing like Holly's; they were more like a boy's or a younger version of his own, rounded and strong.

Chat was out of the question, surely. Low voices could just be made out, back in the lane; they'd be huddled around the car, Alun guessed. He dreaded the appearance of anyone else. Certainly to have the driver, the perpetrator of this carnage, come walking up now with explanations, apologies, recriminations... with anything, just any speech at all: Alun felt if that happened he'd be on the bastard straightaway – it was what he could do to stop Mel having to think about it, having to reply.

'Shush-sh.'

Mel was whispering softly to the horse presumably as she felt each agitation beneath her fingers. 'Shush, Samson.' She breathed the comfortable words but stared straight ahead into the empty road. Beneath the jacket Samson's head jerked.

'I couldn't understand,' Alun said, 'why he kept trying to get up. I mean it must hurt him to...'

'It's not in their nature, to be down like this.'

Another spasm wracked Samson's frame; the rounded mass of dark ribcage and belly, overshadowing the covered head, had taken on the look of something helpless, something blubbery and aquatic now stranded on a dry shore.

'Christ, is he?'

'No,' Mel said.

'I thought then – you know.'

'He's going into shock, I think. A horse is a big thing.' Still not looking, still letting the breeze take the brilliant spirals of hair and irritate her dirty cheek with them. 'They're big so they take a while to die.' (So Samson *was* dying. There was relief in this at least, because Mel's surety meant that there

17

was nothing *he* ought to be doing. There were no actions – messy, difficult, are you up to this? – that if performed might save the horse and if not....) 'They live in their bodies, horses, you know? What their bodies are doing, that's them at that moment. That's where they're at. If you don't ride, you can't understand. It's a good way to be. That's what I try to be – as much as I can. You just are what you're doing and that's it. If you can do that, you can lose all the other stuff – the crap. All the crap with my mum and dad, it's been going on for years and even now – she lives in France now, yeah? With her new bloke. She lives in another country and it can still kick off over nothing. Me... what I'm doing or what she thinks I should be up to. Who owns this really gross painting – that was last thing. He finds it's gone. Two years, then he notices the space on the wall and he's all for going over to get it back because....'

For a moment they could both ignore it and then neither of them could: a siren in the distance but homing in on them, threatening their brittle stasis. Samson heard it, stirred and twitched.

'Shush-sh. I'm not going – if that's the ambulance. I can't leave him till...'

'There's a vet coming,' he said pointlessly.

'I know. Motorbike man said. Thanks.'

A police-car, lights flashing but siren now off, drew up a respectful distance away. The policeman who approached was paunchy and near retirement age by the looks of him, sweating as though attending the scene on foot.

'Oh dear.'

Alun stood up and met him on the road to keep between this new intruding figure and the horse. 'She needs to go to hospital. Broken arm at least, I think – God, I don't know, she could be really hurt. But she won't go till someone's dealt with the horse.'

The policeman glanced down at Samson and up again to Alun. What was the matter with the idiot? What didn't he understand? Alun, his back to Mel, raised his index finger to his own temples. 'OK?'

He nodded. 'The other – I mean the vehicle involved in this, sir. Has it been driven off?'

'Just round the corner. You'll find it in front of my house. But stir up that bloody vet will you?'

They sat for what seemed another couple of hours easily, but was probably only minutes. At one point the policeman came back out of Tatten Lane, talking all the time to a distant agent, removed something from the police-car that Alun couldn't see and went back with it in the direction of Carousel. When a Landrover arrived from the opposite direction to that of the police-car it was Mel who saw it.

'Hello Peter. I was hoping it'd be you.'

'Hello Mel. You um, hanging in there?'

'Yep.'

Peter was tall and wiry and, dressed in a khaki boiler-suit, could have passed for a mechanic, one of those we'll-fix-you-by-the-road-types that Alun had been forced to rely on more than once. Feeling very much the spare part, Alun made space for the vet to kneel between the horse's bent knee and its shrouded head. Peter seemed to ignore the terrible wound from which blood still leaked; he put his hand on the animal's muzzle and pulled at the lower lip. 'Membranes are a poor colour. He's deeply in shock.'

'I know,' Mel said.

'From just what I can see from here,' Peter's contortionist's frame enabled a head-cocked, half-balanced peek into the hole in Samson, 'it looks like lateral head of triceps damage – severe damage... huge amount of tissue loss in the area. Bone fragments might be from the sternum or the ulna or both.' He rocked back and away on his heels but the squeak of rubber boots now failed to set off anything more than a long rattling exhalation from the horse.

'Can you do it now, please?'

'Yes. I think that's the thing to do. Yes. Right, Mel. If you're able to stay there, I'll get my stuff.'

Alun might not have been present: this was to be accomplished by Mel, Peter and Samson, of course. Once Peter had shaved a patch on Samson's neck to insert his lethal injection Alun, more out of curiosity than any distinct purpose, wandered back into Tatten Lane. What met him was an extraordinary scene: across from Carousel on the narrow grass strip it seemed a family picnic was in progress. A young woman sat on a travel-rug, a grizzling baby ignored in her lap while an older, white-haired woman bent to hand her – to hand her very shakily – a steaming plastic top from a thermos flask. The paunchy policeman stood talking to the seated woman whilst being pulled about and interrupted by a small boy who had him by the hand....

So Samson's executioner: not male, as he'd been convinced for absolutely no reason, but one of these ashen-faced, miserable women trying to explain themselves, failing to care for that baby and that little boy who couldn't be much more than Charlie's age...

Who was Charlie!

'Charlie! What are you doing out here?'

20

'Policeman, Daddy! I had his hat!'

In confusion, the policeman turned a suspicious face to Alun, 'So is this your car, sir?'

'What? No! I live here. That's my son – we live in this house and I know the girl. The girl who was hit,' he finished for the benefit of the women.

Charlie's cold little hand was passed across to him without a word.

'I didn't see the accident, just heard it from the garden – then when I went out, there was Mel in the road...'

'That's fine, then. Perhaps you'd like to take your little boy inside and I'll have a word with you when I'm sorted here?'

'I think I'll go back and see how she's doing if it's all the same to you. The vet's...' he looked at the seated woman, who looked away. 'Well, the vet's putting the horse down now. Mel might need someone.'

He regretted it as soon as the words were out. Of course he couldn't take Charlie with him back around that corner, where Samson was dying – or dead, by now – was nothing more than a giant shocking carcass beneath the inadequate cover of a Barbour jacket. But as the policeman was about to argue the point an ambulance, its blue light flashing to the further delight of Charlie, finally arrived. Alun picked the boy up and made to edge past the Merc still half-blocking Carousel's gateway. He should, he knew, offer to take the women and the whimpering baby with him but he clutched the boy hard against his own chest and, 'Come on, Charlie, let's go and get you warmed up,' he said.

'Samson's dead,' Charlie told Holly.

'Who?'

Charlie was curled against her in the chair. Holly's eyes quizzed Alun above the bright, splayed pages of *Billy Penny's Pig*.

'What's he saying?'

'I was going to tell you about it – when he's gone up, though.'

'Oh?'

'Something – not good.'

'Did Charlie see it?'

'Yes, Mummy! Samson's all dead,' Charlie chipped in.

'*No*. Tell you later... What's that you two are reading? What's the story, Charlie?'

Billy Penny was displayed on the cover astride his flying pig and the advantages of being the owner of a pig that could fly thoroughly enlarged upon. Strangely, although the book had been about the house for over a year and he knew the story by rote, so often had it been a bedtime request, only now did Alun notice the name of the book's author: Don Kellett. When he'd been first employed by Durward's as a new graduate in marketing, the company had been run by a Don Kells. Pushing seventy, Don remembered when Durward's had been a *real leather company* – when it had owned tanneries out in Cheshire and Wales, stench-lapped horror-stories of workplaces, cosying up to the friendly neighbourhood abattoirs, that were also no more. It was Don who'd insisted Alun accompany him to the last Durward tannery just before it closed...

...down a scabby little sideroad, it was. The inhabitants of a just-visible council estate had left along its length offerings of mattresses, gaping fridges and carpet off-cuts: fair exchange for the miasma in which they lived. By the time Don nosed the car into the tannery yard, Alun believed the stink of anything could not be more intense – it was overwhelming his ability to choose words, to think even – but it could. Inside. Inside the tannery building the atmosphere was laden to a level of pungency that was intolerable – and yet men stood about in it, men came forward and joked with Don about *sammying* and *perching* in it. Men said, 'All right?' in it to him when he was introduced.

Don Kells: 'Tanning, it's got to be the oldest profession bar one, lad. We were at this before farming.'

Don Kells: 'Nothing like leather, nothing else like it – it'll keep the water out and yet let the vapour through. Seems like it's dead but it still *breathes.*'

Don Kells: 'How long will it last? How long? Well it lasted the beast a lifetime, eh?'

That tannery-stink was back in his nostrils now and on it had risen Don Kells.

The old man would probably be dead. But Alun found he was reluctant to ask Holly though she'd know. Instead he said, 'Isn't that book a bit babyish for Charlie now? He seems to have had it for ages. Shouldn't he be moving on?'

'But we love Billy Penny, don't we Charlie? *Mummy* loves Billy Penny. And we do *wish* we had a flying pig.'

'Did you notice, it's a bloke's written it?'

'Yes, I know.'

'Don Kellett. Reminded me of old Don Kells.'

Holly had no answer it seemed.

'Anyway, what sort of life is that for a bloke, writing baby-books?'

'So what happened?'

'Just like Charlie said, I'm afraid. The horse – it belongs

to, you know... Mel Gethin? I told you about her. She's the girl always stops and lets Charlie feed the horse?' Alun lied, not even sure why he was lying as he did it. 'Well 'bout lunchtime some bitch in a big Merc decides she's turning into the lane and the fact that Mel and this bloody great horse are in the way doesn't slow her down one bit.'

'Christ! Where were you? Is the girl all right?'

'I was gardening with Himself. I heard the crunch. I knew it was going to be bad so I popped him in front of Postman Pat and went out. There's the girl in the road – broken arm, I think but really banged about as well. There's this stupid bloody woman – more worried about the car than anything else by the looks of it. And of course there's this mangled horse. It was obvious they'd have to shoot it – half its chest was hanging out, broken leg – but not dead, that's the bummer.'

'Oh, yuk! So what about the driver?'

'What d'you mean? Police breathalysed her but she hadn't been drinking. Just a naturally rubbish driver.'

'Was she hurt?'

'No. Who cares? I was more into trying to clear up her mess.'

A long pause during which Holly got to her feet and began tidying away Charlie's bright detritus into the pine chest, kept in the corner of the sitting room for just that purpose: somewhere in the series of actions there seemed like a reproach.

'You should have seen it! Mel lying in the road – for a moment I thought she must've had it. Then there's this horse, foaming at the mouth – terrible pain it must have been in. Blood, etc everywhere... Sorry, is this too much detail or something?'

'No. I was listening.' She swept the light fringe from her forehead in a familiar gesture of fatigue. 'I'm glad Charlie... I wondered what he meant about the policeman. He was chattering on about a policeman all the time he was in the bath... I'm just glad that you managed to keep Charlie out of it.'

'Well I did.'

'Yes.'

'Yes.'

'Perhaps you could take him out tomorrow? For a trip somewhere, just to take his mind off anything he *might* have...'

'But I've said, he didn't. Anyway I thought you wanted the path done, before the winter?'

'I do – of course, I do. It's just one day, though. And it's Wednesday – I'll be late tomorrow. I've got that bloke from Bolton coming in. I told you. He's had two shipments from Pakistan he can't use. Full grain for tooling, you see, but what he's getting isn't taking up the water....'

Alun realised something in his face had caused her to tail off.

In the morning the lane outside Carousel seemed untouched by Tuesday's commotion: a solitary bit of broken hawthorn straggled out over the lane. Then he noticed a series of scrapes on the tarmac – marks that disappeared around the corner along the track of the collapsing Samson – and ghoulishly found he must follow them. A magpie flapped up from the spot on the grass where the horse had dropped and died. 'One for sorrow, two for joy,' he said out loud, as though he had Charlie by the hand and with him, instead of back in the kitchen, wide-eyed at Pingu the Penguin, missing his aim with the fingers of toast.

Managing to thorn his hand, he pulled off the broken

branch and threw it into the stubble-field across from the house. Briefly he considered getting out the hose and washing away the gobbets of brown blood on the grass; at the tap he saw the impracticality of the plan. No amount of garden hose was going to stretch from the back door of the garage, across the lawn, through the orchard and all the way out into Wrexham Road.

He was unwilling to touch the flagstones or barrow. The only alternative seemed to be to back the VW out with extra care although, today, there wasn't a single other road user in either direction. The uncomplaining Charlie was soon bundled into the back and they were off – but where?

They'd visit Mel – of course, it was the obvious thing to do – it was a five minute drive in the direction of the town centre and The Old Rectory was unmissable in its own little close next to the church... but when he drew up outside the high brick wall and stared up at five sash windows, most of them with pulled blinds, he failed to switch off the engine, made no move to get out.

'What you think, Charlie? D'you think Mel's there? Or in hospital?'

'Where?' Charlie demanded.

'In there. That's where Mel lives. Is she there?'

'Yes!' Charlie shrieked.

'I don't know – I think they'll have kept her in. Her fath... her daddy's a doctor. They'll have kept her in.' Checking his mirror, letting an elderly woman cross in front of him and gain the pavement and checking again, he drove away. 'Let's go to Pendinas,' he said, 'feed the ducks, eh, Charlie?'

It involved a U-turn on an A-road. Bad start.

Opening and dutifully closing the green gate, he drove up

through the trees and stopped beneath a sign that read DEEP COLD WATER – STAY WELL BACK FROM EDGE. They were on an area of hard standing right next to the reservoir where only fishermen parked but there were no fishermen today though the air was bright and crisp. It had been a 'white-over' again he realised but the landscape had relaxed now under a low Autumn sun. Alun was glad for the emptiness. No old men or the work-shy, glaring at Charlie's high-pitched yells. The water was smooth enough to show the pattern of the far, wooded shore in its depths and a pair of swans paddled across submerged tree-tops. Small islands had poked up through the reservoir's surface since their last visit and gave it now the look of a real lake, a more pleasing place than he recalled. Close in, a handful of mallards gathered into a convoy and made straight for them.

'Bread for ducks,' pleaded Charlie. 'Quick, daddy, quick!'

Of course he had nothing to give the child.

'*Bread*!'

'I'm sorry. Daddy's forgotten it. Nothing for ducks today.'

'Yes, Daddy! Bread. Now.'

Alun walked parallel to the stone edge of the water letting the boy follow. 'Bread, Daddy, bread-daddy, bread-daddy' lessened into low-level whinging – but when he made the mistake of turning around and offering his attention, Charlie seized a piece of fir-tree from the path and lunged at the ducks who had been keeping pace. Once sure of being watched he threw the stick at the bobbing birds. They in turn levered their bodies half out of the water to avoid it and scattered. The missile landed harmlessly but Alun's fury came up like a dark malodorous bubble.

'Don't you do that!' He towered over the child. 'Don't you

27

ever do that! How would you like it, if I threw a stick at you?'

Charlie's eyes grew huge. Any second now the trembling lips would part, the wailing-in-earnest begin.

In one bit of his mind he saw the ridiculousness of it, shouting at the child like that. As a boy, he'd done much the same and worse... and he'd have been older than Charlie – old enough to remember, old enough to know better. Ridiculous. But he didn't reach down for the sobbing child, just taking his hand for a sullen stroll along the path of the earth dam.

There's the place, Charlie, look – look through there and you can watch the water running under the bridge! Look between the sleepers! There is goes. Oh, don't then if you don't want to see....

He watched a long, thin branch – bleached heartwood, white as an arm – waving beneath the surface, seeming to cling to its chosen position, before being swept down from sight. In a few minutes more they were back at the car.

Charlie picked at his lunch and went red-eyed to his nap.

That afternoon Alun had a surprise visitor. He was wheeling the last flagstone along the side of the house when he heard the gate open. By the time he'd lowered the barrow a short, linen-suited man was approaching him, one hand held out, offering to shake. 'Alun, is it?'

'That's right.'

'I'm Cliff Gethin, Mel's father.'

'Oh, right.' Clifford Gethin's hand was small but the grip very firm. 'Nice to meet you. I was going to call to ask how she was but I don't have your number. I was going to walk down to the stables when my son gets up – to ask there. How is she?'

'She's... OK.' Mel's father might be slim and neat and

looking at him out of Mel's dark eyes but there the resemblance ran out. He was completely bald, sunburnt and with a patch of peeling in progress above tinted glasses; the impression was of someone stopping by on his drive back from the airport. 'She's better physically than mentally.' Very much the doctor, that tone, clipped and professional and a place or two higher up the class league than his daughter's soft local burr. 'The arm was a clean break, the rest's just lacerations. Head's fine because I've always made sure she had a damn good hat on it. But the horse, you know?' Alun nodded. 'I gather from Peter it was grim?'

'Shocking.'

'Exactly. Anyway, she said you were a big help and to say thanks.'

'It wasn't anything. You shouldn't have bothered coming over...'

'No bother. I'm just on my way to the stables. Good old Samson! In death, as in life, he left me with bills to settle.'

Brittany had the wife run off to? Hardly seemed far enough.

'I was beginning to think you'd run off as well,' he challenged Holly. It was nearly nine, freezing and black outside. The *as well* went unnoticed.

'I rang. Had to take it easy – there's fog between here and Chester... black ice.'

She was exhausted: it was obvious in her falling back onto the sofa cushions and wriggling half-out of her coat where she sat... in making no move to dash straight up to Charlie.

'Mel's father's Elvis Costello but completely slap-head,' he told her, just after telling her that he thought Charlie might be sickening for something.

'Glasses?'

'Certainly glasses.'

'You didn't take to him?'

'Too right I didn't. His daughter's nearly killed... her horse, well, I won't bore you with going over that again... and all he can talk about is what it's costing him?'

'Well I suppose he's had to pay out a small fortune over the years. But she's OK, you said. Just a broken arm?'

'If that's OK.'

'Oh you know what I mean!' She hauled herself to her feet leaving her impression in the leather of the sofa-seat and the creased silk lining of her coat. 'I'll just look in on him – is it a bug, d'you think? It's not like you to make a big deal of things – the girl getting knocked off her horse, I mean. I couldn't get a cup of tea, could I?'

Perhaps real events could be fashioned through fiction. Perhaps Charlie was coming down with something after all. The child was fretful and uncooperative, seeming to become feverish mid afternoons only to cool and sweeten both days at Holly's walking in. Magically the symptoms vanished for the weekend, returned, as did the nuisance early morning fog, for Monday.

'Take him in to the surgery, will you?'

'I don't think there's anything wrong, Hol.'

'Just to check, then. Oh, it'll probably be nearer seven if the weather's bad.' She swept up her keys from the worktop and had one last scan of the kitchen for anything that still connected her with home, even as her mind wandered out to the car and the journey and beyond the journey. '*Please*. What harm can it do?'

To the young locum Alun said, 'If it was me, I wouldn't be here. My wife's bothered.' Charlie sat on a folded blanket on the examination table, not flushed, not crying, not cowed in the least by his surroundings.

'Well, you were bothered enough to have time off to bring him – let's have a look-see, shall we?'

But the *look-see* revealed nothing other than a touch of inflammation around a late-erupting second molar.

And then there was Mel: when they came out, her brilliant red hair was startling amongst the grey and white heads of those seated around her. So unused was he to seeing her dissociated from Samson, Mel struck him as much smaller than he recalled. A child again, after the adult stoicism he'd witnessed. She was slumped in a corner, her legs drawn in tight and one arm cradling the other in its splint. Only a few days and already the cast, that began at the elbow, was grubby and frayed-looking about the wrist. There was time to note – before she glanced up and recognised him – the darkening of scabs on her hands and the bruise just above her jaw-line, where he'd seen the dirty streak on that day....

'Hello Alun.'

'How you doing?'

'On the mend.'

'You're not having the cast off already?'

'No, worse luck. Fracture clinic in another week.' She stood up and moved toward the door, out of earshot of the assembled sick. 'To be honest I don't know what I'm doing here, really. I'm not sleeping – it's probably just the arm and everything else aching but Dad said – he won't give you anything of course! – he said to come and get something...'

'Right.'

31

'I feel stupid now I'm here.'

'I'm really sorry – about what happened.'

'Yeah.'

He saw her swallow hard but she wasn't going to cry on him. Then – horribly – he felt prickling in his own eyes. He was sorry. *He was so sorry. Just a second sooner or a second later and... it shouldn't have happened.* Only swinging Charlie up into his arms gave him cover to turn away, to say, 'Well, I'm glad I've seen you. I hope... things... work out better. I'm sure your father's right though. You should get something, just to see you through it.'

Charlie slipped over in the surgery car-park: Holly had been right about that black ice. On the dark, dependable-seeming surface his sturdy little legs had buckled and shot him flat onto hands and chin. 'Come on now! I'll rub it, shall I? No? Well don't make a meal of it, then. Be a brave boy. You're not hurt.' It set the tone for another day: the child, miserable, complaining, continually badly-done-to and himself, cajoling, snapping, sticking at none of the tasks he began.

What was wrong?

While he scrabbled in the freezer to exhume fish for the evening meal, while he sanded down a square of panelling in the hall, he asked himself: what the fuck's up, Alun? For three years, almost, he'd cared for Charlie and now for whatever reason – for no reason at all – it was as though they'd fallen out of love. Or what he felt for Charlie was getting shot through with needle all the time, just spike-lets of annoyance that were enough to... but, of course he loved the child and the child loved him.

His son! A new person, different from himself, Alun, certainly but with Alun as the pattern. A son... a virtual copy, as he was of his father – but closer, more adequately expressed. Him and his father – don't even go *there*, Alun – it was going to be a hundred times better than it was with his own father. *And it could only get easier*! As Charlie's boyishness grew, as his gender took a positive form it was Holly that'd find her patience tested. Now when he thought back to the incident at the reservoir it was possible to see it reversed: an omen. The cabinet-scraper slipped from his fingers. Rather than retrieve it he ran up to Charlie's bright-painted room and wakened him with stroking his hair. 'Hello Charlie! Are you going to get up, now? Banana and milk – how about that? And then help Daddy paint that fence?' But the child hadn't slept for long enough: Charlie's eyes flickered and he moaned but he turned again beneath his quilt, clutching it to him with two small fists – and Alun found he had to resist the temptation to prise the bunched material from them, to break their grip.

Meaning to fetch milk for his tea, he found a couple of bottles of Becks in the fridge and sat with them out in the garden, his back against the house wall, his buttocks and legs on the modest expanse of terrace he'd managed to lay in that first flush of summer enthusiasm. It was too cold for sitting but not quite chilly enough to force immediate movement. The sun had pierced the white mist at last, somewhere a blackbird (the only bird he could recognise) was cackling boastfully over its possession of the orchard's rotten produce. When the glow of the first bottle hit and the second was started, he saw Charlie out here again, hooting with delight at the newly-arrived pile of red sand, rolling down from the top, gathering a coating as though it were breadcrumbs....

Unidentifiable weeds sprouted from the near face of the heap now and the thrill of rolling was all worn out.

Somehow the brown, fermenting pulp had got into the house. No – not into the house, *through the house*. 'You've trodden it through the house,' Holly said. 'It must've come in on your boots – it's all up the stairs.' It was the weekend (nearly) again, two days he anticipated with pathetic eagerness and they were going to begin it with a Friday night bicker about this?

Alun walked out into the hall. The pale carpet, left by Carousel's previous owners, now showed the partial-prints of his boots. 'It's in Charlie's room, as well, next to his bed,' Holly called after him, 'I thought it was dog-shit at first...'

'Oh it could've been worse then.'

'But it's rotten apple.'

'I'll get rid of it.'

'How?'

'I don't know – clean it off – hire one of those machines, if that's what it takes.'

Later they ate across from each other without speaking, the kitchen television showing a sluggish documentary about a party of ologists, trekking through some... where on the trail of some lost... thing. Alun reached to click it off.

'You've started on the panelling – in the hall.'

'Yeah.'

'You don't seem to have got very far.'

'Charlie woke up.'

'Oh.'

He could always tell her about Mel, he thought, how he and Charlie'd met Mel in the waiting room – and later on, how the kid at the garage had said she was going to her mother's in France to get over the accident. How everybody in the shop was saying she'd never get on a horse again – and not because she'd lost her nerve (because Mel was a local byword for nerve) but because *they reckon Samson getting killed like that has broken her heart*. But Holly had had no part in the accident, Holly had no part in what went on in Dial Green, though she'd wanted to come and live out here, no part in the house though it'd been her choice. He stayed quiet and cleared their plates away, topped up their glasses....

'You OK?'

'In what way, OK?'

'Oh come off it, Alun! You're not exactly Mr Chatty, are you?' Eyebrows raised she watched him fill his own glass and stop short just at the point of overflowing. 'And your hands are shaking?'

'Perhaps I'm coming down with whatever Charlie's got.'

'But Charlie hasn't got anything – you said.'

'So he hasn't.' He'd genuinely forgotten.

The evening dragged on: Dial Green time, that was the way he thought of it. He'd noticed this weird slowing of the hours in the afternoons and now the infection had spread. The evenings were going the same way, stretched out and thinned. There'd been a schools programme on recently, a twenty-minute Janet-and-John exposé of Relativity with a road, a country lane, pulled out and deformed like chewing gum, never reaching the place the signpost indicated but 'still infinitely long'.

He stood, about to draw the bedroom curtains, but not drawing them, looking down to the dark corner of orchard and beyond to the street light in Wrexham Road. No fog: now that it didn't matter and Holly was safely home it was all icily clear. A single car passed and after a wait, another in the same direction. Back in Dial Green, The Pendy and The Full Moon were emptying out....

35

'*Alun?*' Holly was there, behind him, her warm breasts pressed into his back, the scent of her filling the space between himself and the bay-window, her arms locking across his chest. He guessed she was waiting for him to speak or react in some way but he was under water – too much trouble to contest it – too much of an effort not to sink down – too tired to... to... no, that was Holly – it was Holly always too tired to but making a huge effort to....

She said, 'I didn't know you'd come up to bed.'

'Do you remember that time – we were in the flat and we were just looking out, just like this and we saw the bag-snatch? That boy, swiping the woman's bag? And the big bloke chased him for it?'

'Yes... I remember,' Holly said.

'Whose side were you on? I mean did you hope they caught him or he got away?'

There was a long pause while she rubbed her forehead into the nape of his neck. 'Um-m. Well, the man who was chasing him, I suppose. Yes, of course. The boy had stolen something – and it did look like a *really* good leather bag. Might have been one of ours.'

Jesus Hol, you're meant to be just five years ahead of me, not twenty-five!

Or was she joking? He had no idea. Heart hammering! Suddenly and when he'd asked it for no effort – was it expecting to have to fuel a fight? An escape from something that he didn't know was close? And here was Holly hanging about him, impeding his movements... it was all he could do not to pull her off, push her away. 'I was standing here and I just realised. How I was on the side of the bloke then – but now I wish the kid had made it – got away with it, you know?'

36

'What on earth are you on about?' She let her arms drop and stepped back.

'I don't know. But... something's got to change, Hol.'

'I can see that.'

'Really change.'

'Yes. I think you're right. I can really see it. Can we go to bed, though? I'm dead on my feet. We've got the weekend ahead of us. And nothing's happened – what I mean is, we haven't done anything we can't go back on. We're lucky. There's nothing we can't fix.'

He peeled off his clothes, left them where they fell and got into bed. Later he felt her slip in beside him in the dark and her hand on his shoulder. Later still, her regular breathing. Sleep wouldn't come; instead the scene played out again, this time with Holly not answering his question (or not answering quickly enough) and his turning and shaking her by the shoulders till she cried in pain, till she pleaded, 'I don't know Alun! Whose side do you want me to be on? The kid running away or the bloke after him? Which one?' Her fear of him was new and thrilling. It kept his fingers digging into her thin shoulders. It made him want to keep shaking her as long as it lasted.

It could have so easily gone that way.

Residue

My father was Boris Karloff's double: huge, grey-haired, with deep, cold, Slavic-eyes *and* he had a wicked, unexplained scar across his forehead, as though from botched surgery or some dreadful scientific experiment. One that had failed. Yet he was handsome, to his daughter at least – he must've been. He left her with a taste for men straight out of horror movies.

He was the only member of his family I knew. My mother came with brothers, sisters, nieces, nephews, cousins, second cousins and even, when I was small, parents of her own – and all living within walking or bus-riding distance. But my father was just my father. I and my mother shared the Ellis name but not his origins... and during one particularly bitter marital harmattan (and it must have been a beaut to stand out from the rest) he came up as usual to wish me good-night and added: 'You're all I've got, you know.'

I think he may have patted my foot beneath the eider-down....

Neither of us mentioned it next morning, or ever.

I was nearly into my teens when I found he had a brother. It happened strangely, as did everything to do with him. Of course you never see it at the time: the house rules are the only imaginable rules when the house is your home.

Neighbours – some remote relatives of my mother's cousin, Peggy – heard the news from their family in the South. As was the way in Saltney village then, one of them walked straight in: Saturday morning radio enlightening nobody in particular... except perhaps an elderly budgie as it crooned to its mirror. My mother was hanging out washing, my father in the dining-room, the racing pages spread out before him. Me? What would I ever be doing but watching it all? The Invisible Girl.

'Gwil,' said Mrs Bennion (who might have been my mother's cousin Peggy's aunt by marriage or something even more tenuous) 'Gwil, did you know that Robert... that your brother Robert had died? Down in Cardiff?'

'Has he?' my father asked.

'Hadn't you heard?'

'No.'

'Oh, yes. I thought you might not have. A couple of weeks ago. At least. Heart attack. What would he've been? Fifty?' She enquired in the tone of someone settling an argument – or who had a bet on.

'About that,' my father said.

'Right – I thought as much. No big age, though. Pity, eh?'

And that was it. My mother didn't utter a word. The neighbour was taken with embarrassment – though it could so easily have been boredom – and left. My father's interest in the runners and riders at Chepstow grew from good to firm. He squinted at the blurred lists, detailing every known recorded facet of brief equine lives and it seemed he had to pick the paper up now so that it covered his face – just to make out who'd been placed, who'd failed to start, who'd thrown its jockey... who'd fallen at the last.

We left him and slipped out to the line and whispered over the revelation as we positioned five perfectly-spaced wooden pegs in the candy-striped flannelette. Even in bereavement my mother's strict sheet, pillow-case, pillow-case, sheet series could not be interrupted.

'I never knew Dad had a brother!'

'Oh, mm-m,' she mumbled through a mouthful of wood.

'Who?'

'Robert – the youngest. By two or three years. There'd *been* a sister but...'

'Younger than Dad – and he's dead! Did you ever meet him?'

'Meet him? No. Me, meet Robert? How would I meet him?'

Forty-seven, Sandy Lane – we should've had a blue plaque stuck up there on the pebble-dash, between the mock-Gothic porch and the little leaded light: 'Forty-seven, Sandy Lane, Saltney, Flintshire. Birthplace of the Unanswerable Question.'

Sundays were always tense. We felt restless and resentful at the imposed leisure and since my revolt over Chapel attendance, I was as bad as the other two. Once the dinner was produced and cleared – my father prepared vegetables, mother meat – no one was sure what to do with the carcase of a workless day... chew over it in aggrieved silence or pick a fight? Reading sometimes came in third: a proper novel for her, an Edgar Wallace or a Western for him, H G Wells for me or Arthur C Clarke... Isaac Asimov, Brian Aldiss – anything that wasn't about real life and preferably set in another solar system. A planet full of aliens was favourite – no human-beings at all. I'd just finished *The War of the Worlds* and had seen my side (the Martians) comprehensively defeated.

The seeds from the blackberry and apple pie still lodged between my teeth, I swept up the last of the crumbs and the porcelain cow that covered a hard pat of Stork margarine. This was my escape ticket from the room.

Not a good choice.

'Do you know how they make butter?' my father demanded.

My mother was wrestling with the *News of The World*. We heard a snort from behind THE VICAR AND THE LADY DOC-TOR – WHAT THE BISHOP DIDN'T KNOW!

That left me.

'How do they make butter?' I asked him.

'I'll show you – come on.'

From the fridge he produced the last pint of unopened milk.

'We need something to churn it – it has to go round and round to make it stick together... something with a lid.'

'What sort of something?'

'A bottle – that should be OK.'

The kitchen cupboard had bottles all right – bottles of PLJ lemon juice (my mother must've been slimming again and not letting on), Heinz Salad Cream, strawberry syrup for putting on puddings and olive oil for putting on burns... milk of magnesia... and Daddies Sauce with a couple of inches of brown gloop in the bottom and a tawny, crusted top.

42

'This'll do,' he said and emptied out the contents under the hot tap. I scrubbed the cap with the nail brush and we half-filled the squat little container, spilling as much again onto the draining-board. Neither of us thought to wipe it up.

I perched on a stool and, under direction, spun the bottle, its neck against my palm. 'Nothing's happening, Dad.'

'Not yet. It takes a long, long time. Churning the butter – that's what it's called.'

'Why not turning? Churning's just turning. What d'you need another word for when...'

'Because you just do! It's always been called churning. Give it here!'

He snatched it from my hands and let it revolve in his larger, calloused fingers with their skin–memories of cuts and blisters and bright steel slivers and the unforgiving teeth of saws. 'When we were boys – a lot younger than you – Robert and I'd churn the butter. That'd be our job.'

This was a *real* Tale of Wonder. He had never once let slip a reference to, a story about, an admission concerning his childhood – and now here it was, that other life, flashing into view: Dad as a boy with a younger boy beside him, churning the butter.

Time travel.

'Did you live on a farm, then?'

It was hard to picture my father and this ghostly uncle, this doomed Robert, amidst the fields of clover and grazing animals of Cissy Morris's farm... which was at the end of Sandy Lane and the only one I knew.

A countryman? – my father, whose mobile hands showed only the record of a forty-year love affair with the machine?

'Did you, Dad, did you live on a farm?'

'Not really... it was, er...' his eyes were focused somewhere deep inside the tidal milk. 'We'd pick the fruit in season – gooseberries were the worst, you'd come home like a pin-cushion – shift hay for the cows, up to your knees in mud. Best was taking the horses to the forge. It was hard work, I know that.'

He looked up and there was no smile to soften the accusation: 'You... you don't know you're born.'

In the Daddies Sauce bottle the butter failed to form. I watched for a minute longer. What was I meant to do? *Will* it to appear, perhaps – but how? By telekinesis? Just like George Fotheringay produced a perfectly cooked goose-egg out of nowhere in *The Man Who Could Work Miracles*. And what a stupid waste of his powers that had been, whereas if I could've worked miracles, there was no end to the useful, remedial things I could've done, like turning us all into a normal family with a record player and an Uncle Robert who came around and noticed I'd had my plaits cut off and asked if I was better at Welsh or French.

The milk stayed milk.

There was a crackle of paper from the next room. 'Richard Burton and Elizabeth Taylor have split up again,' my mother thought we ought to know. 'I wonder if he'll let her keep that ring?'

Dad and I had no opinion.

The milk stayed milk.

Fingers that had once been pin-cushions for gooseberry thorns, that had locked on the tight sisal corset of a baled breakfast for cows now, deftly, rhythmically spun the bottle – and over and over, ebbing and flowing, the milk stayed milk.

'Mair's got the new Abba single,' I just had to mention –
and I fancied I heard my mother's laugh.

'Horses?' said Mair when I told her. 'How old is your Dad?'
I'd never wondered but now I knew. 'More than fifty,' I
said, 'and his brother's already dead. He must be old. They
had horses... to pull things.'

'*I bin through the desert on a horse with no name,*' Mair
sang as we cavorted around the room she shared with two
other sisters. The Abba single had turned out to be no more
than a mirage. '*It felt good to get out of the rain.*'

Horses. On a farm, where boys called Gwilym and Robert
picked fruit and fed cattle up to their knees in mud... and rode
bare-back to the forge, as a treat.

Time travel.

Sunday evening, round about six, was the most depressing
hour to return to our place – religious warbling on the box and
Mum, hot and martyred, ironing all our stuff for the week's
imminent kick-off. She stared at me, sourly, through a cloud
of steam rising from my white school blouse. 'You've been
long enough. I though you'd left home. Has Mair's gran come
out of hospit...?'

'Look!' Dad brandished the sauce bottle in triumph.
Within its murky contents a pale buttery blob about the size of
a walnut had materialised. We hurried to the sink. 'Fetch a
cracker while I get it out,' he said.

But the butter wouldn't come out. It lodged in the slender
glass neck and could only be extracted a knife-full at a time.
Dad handed it over for me to scrape onto my tongue.

'Go on.'

'You really made butter, Dad?'

'Go on – eat it.'

It didn't taste like butter. It felt like butter, soft and rich and warm from his hands but it tasted... it tasted of... 'Oh-h, ugh!'

'What's the matter?'

In the corner the iron froze in mid-air, poised over one leg of my father's works–issue blue overalls.

'It tastes of something... oh, like vinegar?... it tastes of sauce, Dad!' I wiped my lips to be rid of the sharp, greasy residue. 'You didn't wash the bottle out properly. All you can taste is sauce.'

He raised the knife and sniffed. 'You're right. I can smell it now.'

He let the grey liquid run into the sink and bowled the sauce bottle with its picture of a nineteen-fifties daddy neatly into the bin. In the pits of his Boris Karloff eyes lurked the experimenter's misery and the monster's despair.

'We used to carry the butter-milk out to the pig trough,' he said. 'Robert and me.'

Living in Hope

There was never one thing Mabli could point to and say, 'That's it – I'm not taking any more.'

Each single event lacked the juice. There was never *quite* enough to fuel the explosive pop that would've had everyone else in the office pausing at their keyboards, silent mid-sentence, unmindful of the photocopier's flashing lantern, waiting for the scene they hoped for, prayed for, longed to see acted out.

Never one thing.

'Got the Evans quote ready?' Carol would ask. 'I'd like a look.'

'You said Friday.'

'I don't think so.'

'Yes, you said Friday. Remember?' Mabli knew that a slight smile – unwanted, unmeant – would be playing now about her own lips. 'Alex came in and...' a frantic scanning of

47

the bright, open-plan work-space would, of course, reveal an unaccountably absent Alex, 'and you said to let him help, so he could learn how to... um... and I said...'

'So it's not ready?'

'Not yet, no.'

'Oh well, Friday'll have to do.' Carol had a technique for ensuring that all those present heard her have the last word. She'd walk away, very casually, the bunched calves of her shapely legs apparently in retreat. She seemed to transfer her interest to some other activity, some other victim altogether. And then over one shoulder – and immediately before the blessed relief of her closing door – 'Just this once, Mabli,' she'd say.

And although it was only Wednesday and she had more pressing tasks to perform, Mabli would find, 'Dear Reverend Evans,' coming up onto her screen, 'You enquired recently about the costs involved in the private publication of your memoir *A Half-Century in Hope*. I am so sorry that Seren, Parthian, Gomer and Honno Women's Press have shown so little interest in your work. Having examined the manuscript, I take pleasure in enclosing Proberts Printing's estimate for one hundred copies....'

Yet time off – away from Proberts – was somehow the worst. Six, seven o'clock as the dark drew in she'd find herself thinking: It's night now, black outside and it'll still be black when I wake up and nearly black when I catch the bus and only truly light when I get there and she'll be... and it'll go on and on for this week and another week until...

'You have to leave,' Gary said.

'Can't do that.'

'Why not?'

Why not, she wondered. 'Em, because, well – why should I? It's a nice place. I used to really like it.'

'It *used* to be a nice place,' Gary corrected. 'You used to enjoy it. Past tense. I mean it's not as if...' he overrode her attempts to butt in, 'it's not as if it can get any better, is it? The old man's retired. Carol's the boss now. She's family. She's not going to move on.'

'I know.'

But when she was at her desk what Gary had said – and all the other things in the same vein that Gary had said – these seemed to be... if not less true, then less convincing. It was at home she was most miserable, most achingly bereaved. At her desk in Proberts... at her beech-effect work-station, sitting back in her ergonomically-designed chair and by the light of her glare-free lamp (all Carol's introductions) her mouth might be arid and her underarms moist, but she was doing her job. She was working at something she enjoyed – alongside Mavis and Lynn and Alex and even Nora with her tattoos and silver rings and damson love-bites, Nora who drove the delivery van in her biker-leathers and who was older than Mavis, when Mavis had been admitting to forty-nine for the three years Mabli had been at Proberts. 'Dear Reverend Evans,' she wrote, 'Thank-you for your prompt reply. I am pleased that you have accepted our quotation for the printing of your book *A Half-Century in Hope* – and I'm sure it will be a great success locally. Perhaps you would like to call in one day next week so that we can go through the photographs you mention and decide on a suitable cover design?'

'I think I'll see our literary vicar,' Carol said.

'Fine,' Mabli said.

'Perhaps you could chase up those fliers for the alarm company?'

'They're on the van. Nora will...'

'They're no good on the van, Mabli. Mr Harris will be round for them – any time.'

'But nobody told me.'

'Nobody *told* you,' Carol's voice thickened with mock-concern. 'Oh dear.' Her brown eyes, always brilliant with some strong, surface emotion rolled upward, towards a polystyrene ceiling. 'Well, perhaps you will *tell* Mr Harris when he turns up why his two thousand leaflets are on their way to bloody Wrexham, eh?'

As soon as Carol's dorsal fin had disappeared below the glass half of the partition wall, Mavis scuttled over with tissues. 'Don't mind it, chuck,' she said.

'Just jealous – that's her problem,' Alex suggested, slipping unregarded by the other three into a favourite fantasy universe of competing females.

'What have I done, Mavis?'

Mavis shook her head. 'Nothing. You haven't done anything. It's just... how she is.'

I have lived in Hope over fifty years, the Reverend Evans had begun, *even though I was born in Caergwrle.* It was an old joke about the two adjacent villages, one with its English name, one with its Welsh. The proofs lay scattered across the desk together with a deck of amateurish, black and white snaps: *My predecessor, the Reverend Selyf Popple, Sunday School Outing to Llangollen, 1959* etc, etc.

Carol's interest in the cleric's reminiscences had evaporated... had never existed, apparently. 'Me? See him? No! Books in English down to you, Mabli, books in Welsh to Lynn.'

50

'I can do both, actually. '

'Oh, did you hear that, Lynn?' Carol called across to where Proberts' longest-serving employee toiled over *Fron Goch*, an historical pamphlet by a deranged local teacher. 'Hear that? Mabli says I can sack you now.'

Lynn was a reserved though pleasant enough woman in her forties; she favoured them both with a non-committal nod.

'I didn't say that!' Mabli pleaded but Carol's laughter was all the response – Lynn had returned to that remote hillside of *Fron Goch* where a Celtic princess was, at that very moment, being ritually strangled.

'Of course,' Gary said, 'she wouldn't get away with it in a proper company.'

'Proberts is a proper company.'

'I mean, you know, a real one – not a family firm. They'd have an anti-bullying policy. At our place...'

'You work for the council,' Mabli pointed out. 'Housing office? That's not a company. You don't have to worry about making money – you just spend other people's.'

'But I was just saying that if it was run on proper lines...'

'You don't have to worry about putting in the lowest tender for some... for some coffee-shop menus... when the new place in town is snapping at every bit of work there is. And Carol Bloody Probert is there...'

'I've told you,' he said, 'give it up.'

'Oh, right,' said Mabli, 'and how'll we keep going, then? This place – all the bills? Oh but of course – you can get us a council flat, back on the estate.'

And Gary spent his first night ever on an old sofa (Mabli's mother's throw-out) and hobbled around the housing office next morning with a ricked back and resentful glare –

while Mabli sat prickly-eyed over the Reverend Evans' gentle prose.

...and hardly had I recovered from the surprise and delight of being entrusted with my first ever parish than another momentous event occurred. I was introduced by Mr Meurig Lloyd, the choirmaster of our little church, to his beautiful daughter Ruth who, within a few short years, would consent to become my beloved wife.

'Any good?' Alex asked over her shoulder.

'Well, you know...'

'Any sex and violence?'

Mabli shook her head. 'There's a postmistress here got minor injuries when an escaped ram knocked her off her bike in Kiln Lane. There's a photo of the lady in uniform – and I've got the ram, somewhere – Noddy, he was called. I've got him... yes, grazing in a front garden. Want a look?'

'No thanks,' Alex said. 'It'll get me too excited.'

'Oh, Mabli!' Carol – neat, small, unnoticed – was suddenly amongst them, 'If you've finished with your toy-boy, could I have him now? Just for a bit of work before lunchtime.'

Later as they were sitting, still with the sulphurous scent of egg batches in the air and considering a top-up for the cooling coffees, the outer door was flung open with such force the top pane shattered against the side wall. It had said *Proberts – Printers and Publishers Est – 1951* and now lozenges of old, brittle glass with numbers or letters were scattered like puzzle pieces. A young man – no more than seventeen by the look of his smooth, pale face – literally shot into the office, halted just as suddenly and stared around, as though expecting to find himself in some completely other interior. Mavis, as the mother of several grown-up sons, was the first on her feet.

'What the bloody hell's going on here? What d'you think you're doing?'

The boy looked from face to face, reminding Mabli of a dog tied up outside a shop, scanning each passer-by for its owner. If he'd heard Mavis he showed no sign. 'I want her,' he said. 'And a key. Somebody's stolen my key.'

'Look love,' Mavis said, not unkindly, 'I don't know what's the matter but you can't just come in here.' She gave Mabli and Alex a slight hand-gesture that said *careful* bilingually. But Lynn, amazingly, had decided this was nothing to do with her... was fixated on her screen.

'I want a key,' the boy repeated. There was a new tone in the voice now: an end to patience... and he switched from still to turbulent in a instant, circling the room, picking up any loose object he could find – pens, a stapler, three biscuits in cellophane – and dropping them onto the carpet tiles. He sent a plastic cup full of paperclips flying, using the back of his hand like a ping-pong bat. But Alex's bar of chocolate he seemed to recognise and slipped into the pocket of his grubby combats.

'Hang about!' said Alex.

'I want her-r!' the boy shouted and as though empowered by his own bellow pulled a drawer from an empty desk and smashed it against the frame.

'Now look, you,' Alex said.

'Don't!' Mavis cautioned.

Lynn, whose keyboard was at that moment snatched from beneath her raised fingers and flung down, said nothing at all.

'I'd better call... somebody, you know,' Mabli whispered.

'*No – don't do that.*'

Carol (with a startled rep from the card suppliers at her shoulder) crunched across the broken shards, ground the broken biscuits into the floor and took the intruder by one shoulder. 'Bradley,' she said, 'what are you doing here?'

'I just want a key,' he said.

'Oh, I get it.'

Mabli was fascinated. This was a Carol that she had never seen. Scared, as they all were, she had become gentle. She ran a perfectly manicured little claw of a hand up and down the boy's arm, as though warming a chilled child. 'Never mind about any old key... How did you manage to come here? No – doesn't matter, now. Oh, *Bradley*.'

Bradley did not respond to his name. Mabli realised why he'd appeared dog-like. The boy's eyes were large and shining – and brown. With an irritable movement he shook Carol off, shouting, 'I just want a key to the house, you cow!' and to the rest of them, as though in appeal, he screamed, 'She won't give me a key to my own fuckin' house.'

'*Bradley*! That's enough now. You have to earn it, Bradley. You know what happened when you had one, you...'

He called her 'a fucking bitch' and 'cunt' – a word Mabli never heard spoken out loud in real life, not at Proberts Printing nor at home with Gary, nor even at Quiz Night at The Pendy Arms.

He turned to run out, then, almost as an afterthought dropping Carol to her knees with a fist in the chest. She made a soft little indeterminate noise. And then no noise at all.

Relieved of Bradley's presence and threat, the others found themselves intensely embarrassed. Once Carol had got to her feet – the growing white circles in her black tights flecked with blood, the shifted lipstick and mascara turning her wet face into a clown's mask – the card supplier's rep managed to slink away with a mumbled excuse. Mabli began picking through the debris. In one hand she held a shard of glass with its perfectly centred *Est*, in the other a cracked Millennium mug. Alex retrieved Lynn's keyboard... pretended to examine it.

'All right, love?' Mavis asked. 'I could drive you home, if you like.'

Carol seemed actually to consider it before replying. 'Er, no. No, I'll... I'll pop over to Mum and Dad's now, I think.' She brushed away the brilliant needles clinging to the hem of her pencil skirt. 'Thank-you Mavis. You can all just... clear up and... go home yourselves. Yes... that'll be... all right.'

'What on earth was that?' Mabli asked when she'd gone.

Lynn broke the silence. 'That was Bradley – Carol's boy.'

'I never knew she had a son,' said Mavis. 'Never any sign of a man...'

'She was just a girl, herself.'

'And what's his problem?' – this from Alex, retrospectively angry.

But that was as much as they were going to get out of Lynn.

'Drugs, isn't it?' Mabli suggested.

Lynn looked away.

A Half-Century in Hope, laminated and bound, sat in two fifty-book packages on the stock tables. On Mabli's desk a gash copy lay open at the final page: *Many of the characters that have filled out this short memoir are no more – and for that reason the writing of it has been a bitter-sweet experience. But one thing must be obvious to even the most casual reader. It has been my privilege to live and work amongst those whom I genuinely respect and care for...*

55

It was Carol's first appearance in a week.

'The Evans' book?' she asked.

'All done,' said Mabli.

'We could – I mean, have you suggested he tries to get it reviewed?'

'*Flintshire Leader*, Gareth at *The Vale Advertiser* – done them.'

Carol's gaze was brilliant and unsettling as ever, the irises a fraudulent warm sorrel. But her lips were pale, unaccentuated... a crustacean of a cold-sore already well-formed at the side of her mouth.

'And the quote for Hill and Jenkins? Needs to be in by the tenth.' The words came out as sharp, painful – as though the sore was nipping at anything, any word, any sentence, that passed its way.

'Needs to be in by the seventeenth,' said Mabli, 'if you care to check.'

'No, no,' said Carol, 'I'm sure you're right.'

All the Rest

The son that had brought them together couldn't make the funeral. Bumming lifts somewhere in Queensland, he still didn't know of his mother's death, even at this latest of stages: the coffin and mourners passing with difficulty over the broken limestone pavement before Graigfawr United Reformed Church.

Ahead, Denzil, the new widower, stumbled and Ben's hand just caught him under the elbow, just stopped him going down. And then something terrible happened. It was one of those things that people present would always remember, long after the funereal details had been absorbed into that general mish-mash of stored similar events. Ben fell himself. With a momentum he shouldn't have possessed he lurched, spun, shoulder-charged an elderly woman (Iris... Butler, yes) who ricocheted onto the sodden grass... while he came to rest sprawled behind Sandy's coffin.

Mercifully the bearers continued. Denzil and Uncle Tom hauled him upright.

'You go in,' he said thickly. His mouth seemed to be filling with brine. His wrists throbbed. The acid yellow of the ragwort poking up through the stones – so bright, so inoffensive a moment before – now, when his eyes rested on it in shame, induced a liquid nausea behind his ribs.

'Bloody hell, Ben,' Uncle Tom laughed when they were standing alone, 'you look worse than...'

'Don't say it.'

'No, well... here,' he handed across a crisp white hand-kerchief, 'do your best with this. Christ you're a mess – your mouth's all cut.'

'I know.'

'You'll be all right?'

'Fine. Yeah. Go on. I'll follow you.'

The Day Thou Gavest Lord Is Ended drew Uncle Tom, a superb baritone, through the four-centred arch like the promise of... Ben couldn't imagine what would motivate his red-faced uncle. More money? He'd taken over the family auctioneers when he and Denzil had refused – and had made what passed for a fortune on the Welsh Borders.

Hurriedly he fitted into his seat beside Denzil. His brother was bent forward, head in hand, the weight taken on the balls of the feet – and for a horrible moment Ben feared he was close to collapse. But no – he was displaying that 'at prayer' posture required to show that some sort of weird communications channel had been opened with a non-existent being – a being that the majority of those in chapel viewed with the same amused tolerance they treated Father Christmas.

And the place was *packed* – packed for gregarious, fun-loving Sandy... it sounded like an item from a contact magazine... blonde, non-smoker, GSOH – I have been told I look young for my age! – loves children, cinema, eating out....

Sociable even in death.

He found he was holding a little white booklet: *In loving memory of Sandra Hopkins, beloved wife of Denzil and mother of Huw, who fell asleep on Saturday 24th March 2002, aged forty-nine.*

Sandra not Sandy – his parents would've approved the formality.

...would've loved the occasion since they'd hated the coffin's contents.

They stood and sat and stood again – God, his knees were stiffening where they'd hit the flags, his lip was swelling – and then they were singing, Uncle Tom's rich and powerful tones drawing all the lesser voices up to the plain wooden rafters. *The Lor-ord's my shepherd I'll not want, He ma-akes me down to lie-e, In pa-astures green; he lea-ee-deth me-ee–* was it quite decent to be giving such a faultless performance – such a lyrical, bel canto performance – at a funeral?

Denzil's navy blue shoulders heaved, his face set in new deep lines.

Our Father who art not in Heaven, Ben prayed, forgive me for having seen my brother's wife naked.

He makes me down to lie... In pastures green he leadeth me.

Anything, or almost anything, could reinvent that day.

The shadowless warmth.

The silent, green midday.

At the end of the garden of Stone Lodge the rhododendrons clustered around a grass tennis court in six-foot sweeping bays. But it was high summer. The purple flowers were a brown shrivelled memory and shiny new leaves all that was left to brighten the dusty foliage. Beneath, everything was dry and parched.

Something had happened at school.

Strange how – when every other detail of that time was sharp and complete – he could never recall what had incited the unexpected half-holiday.

Was it fractured pipes that had flooded all of the lower classrooms? That must surely have been associated with winter cold... for whatever reason it was a fine July day and here he was, eleven years old, satchel swinging, shirt hanging loose, running along the lane, up the seven steps and through rose-beds made powerfully fragrant by heat.

The house had been empty. Only Keeler, his mother's ancient corgi, drowsed in a square of parquet on the hall floor. 'You're cooked,' he had said to it (his mother's phrase) burying his hands in the burning fur... and then it was blazer around the slim point of the newel post, cap skidding across the polished wood-blocks like a puck and out into the garden.

It was as though the Earth had been emptied.

The newly cut lawn was unpicked over by blackbird or thrush, and the abandoned mower lay coated in sticky, pungent clippings, just starting to bake. The fountain was turned off – and if golden carp still lingered in the pond they were clouded in its depths.

Stored energy from the crazy paving caressed his bare legs, made him need to, want to, move. He ran up and back across the terrace, missing every crack with the perfect precision of measured hops, the last one taking him onto the path, heading for the scarlet glow of the vine-house where an old, sweet grape vied for space with his father's geraniums. Here he could search for toads beneath the staging and torment them into inflating their baggy bodies or... but somehow he was carried past... past the water butt, past the walled compost heap where on Tuesdays old Mr Parry rested his buttocks and smoked roll-your-owns, thin as drinking straws, past the vegetable plot in full production and on to....

The net sagged with Denzil's jersey and a bright-as-Smarties, multi-coloured jacket, that he'd never seen before. Two rackets and a brand new ball lay beside it. Denzil and Sandy were not twenty feet away – she completely naked on the bed of her own cotton dress, he stripped to the waist but with cricket whites loose around his hips, grass-stained tennis shoes showing grimy soles. They lay in the protective curve of the rhododendron bushes, so close the foliage rattled in rhythmic sympathy. Sandy's arms and legs were creamy tentacles around his brother's torso and he was whispering some thing – some word – over and over in time to the movement. It sounded like 'oyster'. Could it be oyster?

When Sandy's face turned toward him, Ben saw her eyes were bound with a dark band – Denzil's college tie.

The shock of that tie was a gradual one: at eleven it had meant less than the bare flesh (as Denzil had drawn back one of Sandy's large, mobile breasts fell into view with a brown nipple that in his boy's imagination should've been ruby or bright pink)... the bare flesh and the act of penetration, only recently heard about and hardly believed in. Now it occupied his inner eye, even as he took the gin-and-tonic from his brother's hand with his own raw fingers.

'How's Huw getting on at Merton?'

'Good. Still good. Lot different, of course, from when I was... I told him....'

Denzil couldn't say more, remembering, presumably, what he still had to tell the absent Huw.

They were left speechless with the Oxonabilia between them: the oar resting in its brackets above the bookcase and the photographs... Huw, dinner-jacketed and laughing, a pretty girl on his arm... an old black-and-white of Denzil touching down in the Iffley Road mud one freezing afternoon, his face stiff with intent.

'Come and have a breather, Den. Megan's got this lot sorted.'

'I will – I just need to–'

'You don't need to do anything. Come on.'

The mystical status conferred by grief opened a path through the crowded room. There was only one spot to make for in the mean little outside patch, a set of teak table and chairs that almost filled the lawn.

'Do you ever miss the old house?'

'God, no. This does us fine. Everything bright and modern – that's what Sandy likes. Low maintenance.'

I saw you, Ben wanted to say, in the grass... in the garden, the sun on your back. You, the shining boy, everybody's hero... Denzil, the genius loci of Stone Lodge. Mother and Father and me and the aunties and uncles and the big noisy friends and even the teachers from that damn school I had to follow you to – we all worshipped at your shrine.

Denzil, shagging (that's what he'd called it at eleven years old) Denzil shagging the woman from the pub, the woman from behind the bar.

Woman.

'How old is she?' he could still hear his mother demand. (He could hear but couldn't see her say it and must've been in hiding). 'Thirty? Thirty is she?'

'Twenty-six,' Denzil had replied, nothing in his voice.

'Twenty-six? A woman of twenty-six goes and gets herself...'

'Sandy. That's her name.'

'A woman of twenty-six doesn't get like... this by accident. You mark my words. She knew what she was doing. She...'

'Sandy.'

'It's a trap. Just a trap for you. Your life – ruined.'

'It's a baby,' Denzil had said. 'We need to get married. Soon as we can.'

And Mother had sobbed – all over the house... in her room, over meals, dead-heading the roses, grooming the corgi, picking away at her favourite bits of Schumann on the fine-toned upright in the morning room – sobbed as though *she* were a girl made pregnant and then abandoned by the handsomest buck on the Welsh Borders. Sobbed and sobbed... right up until and including the Bergmanesque morning Denzil and Father and Uncle Tom and cousin Megan had gone all the way over to Shrewsbury and returned with Sandy as the family's newest member.

To be joined in four or five months by Huw.

'They never took to her, you know. Specially the old girl.'

'I know,' Ben said. 'But that can't matter now, surely? I thought it was very touching, all the... kids from your year group in the church.' He had almost said boys but the grey-clad contingent was half-female.

'It does matter,' Denzil snapped. His hands were fists that looked harder than teak on the teak tabletop. His face flushed the colour of a brick, causing Ben to wonder how many drinks ahead he might be. 'It didn't while Sandy was here, but it does again now... Specially Mother. She could be a real bitch.'

They spoke of the elderly pair as though deceased, while at that very moment they were enjoying a hedonistic and active retirement in Llandudno.

'They wanted to come, you know.'

'I know they did,' Ben said.

'I told them not to bother, with the drive and everything.'

'I know.'

They'd left the glazed doors ajar. Familiar voices could be dissected out of the subdued murmur. Megan's 'I'm making a fresh pot, *cariad*, don't drink that.' Uncle Tom's 'No! They still live in Oswestry – saw *him* at Bangor-on-Dee... or was it Chester? I've definitely seen him this year. Gave me a tip and the bugger's still running!' Guilty laughter fell heavily out onto the patio.

'Uncle Tom's had a couple.'

It was the wrong thing.

'I don't mind,' Denzil said defensively. (Ben realised he'd just crossed some invisible line. Partitioning what from what, he wondered.) 'He was very fond of Sandy.' (Ah, that from that.)

So, on the one hand there was Denzil and Uncle Tom and Huw, of course, and Megan in all likelihood, and on the other there was Mother and Father and *himself*?

Uncle Tom was very fond of Sandy, was he? What could he say in reply? So was I? Fond of Sandy – robust and unremarkable in the remains of her youth, coarsening into middle-age. He wasn't fond of Sandy.

64

So were *we*? 'Emma was...' he began.

'Mm?'

'Emma was really sorry not to be able to... be here.'

'Yes.'

'You should come down and stay for a bit – when you can.'

'Yes.'

Megan appeared with a small white plate full of small white sandwiches, each with its pink or green or yellowish stripe. His cousin was broader in the hips now, hair touched with grey... but her face was pretty much that of the girl who'd set off for Shrewsbury one morning with Father and Uncle Tom – and Denzil wearing his first ever suit and Merton tie.

I saw her, Denzil, he wanted to say – saw Sandy who worked behind the bar wrapped around you – my first naked woman. The sky and the court and the tennis ball you never hit... and her jacket, all picture-postcard bright. You never forget it, your first naked woman, and this one was blindfolded with your college tie.

Definitely a woman. Cruelly he'd added up the years as he'd sat in church, only half-listening to the 'all those who knew her will remember some small example of her kindness, sense of humour, her love of life' stuff droning on in the background. Not her honesty. It was a sour thought. Sandy who'd 'fallen asleep' aged forty-nine, had been twenty eight on that hot July day.

Gradually they filtered out in ones and twos: Uncle Tom, checking his florid old face as he approached to clap Denzil's shoulder and raise his eyebrows, just barely, to Ben. Several unknown friends of his dead sister-in-law came and went, slipping off now to attend to children's teas. The headmaster from Denzil's school had hung on a surprisingly long time and managed to outstay the decrepit, Welsh-speaking contingent. Denzil got to his feet to shake hands. He looked younger than Denzil – a pompous little prick, Ben had him down for. 'You're an old boy, too, I believe?' he said to Ben.

'That's right.'

'Are you in teaching as well?'

'I work in television. I produce drama.'

'Really? Denzil has...'

Kept this quiet, Ben filled in for him.

'Denzil has mentioned it, I think. Perhaps you could... Perhaps we'll meet again, at a less tragic...'

Only Megan and Iris Butler – recovered from his high tackle outside the church – were left now, crossing backward and forwards in front of the patio doors as they collected the debris of the funeral baked meats. A low-octane tragedy it was turning out.

'Is there somewhere we could walk, Den?'

They made their way through a wooden-lap gate that opened seamlessly in the wooden-lap fence. It led them out onto a gravelled footpath skirting a dozen other hideous, barely-detached boxes. The big village/small town of Graigfawr spread up the hill ahead and at its apex, amidst the evergreens, the huge, turn-of-the-last-century ugliness of Graig School – where a resentful colleague of Denzil's would be glancing at his or her watch, wondering how much he or she could decently shave off a geography class forced on him or her by an inconsiderate, mid-term death.

'Christ,' Denzil said, looking up at the school.

Without needing to say, they turned in the direction of Stone Lodge. It was a pretty enough shot ahead – early summer

66

greens, with a half-timbered cottage set back behind its shrubbery, the whole thing spoiled at the far side by an asbestos garage and overhead power lines.

12. EXT. ENTRANCE TO STONE LANE – MIDDAY
BEN is making his way home, pulling at his school uniform collar, swinging a black canvas school bag at the hedgerows. He passes a half-timbered cottage at the front of which a woman kneels, weeding a border. Her neck-line sags revealing a sweat-shiny cleavage.

> WOMAN
> *You're out early, Ben. Not well, is it?*
> BEN
> *Gas leak... you could smell it in the library.*
> *Sent us all home. The school might blow up.*

WOMAN laughing and leaning even further forward to resume work.

> WOMAN
> *Here's hoping, eh?*

CUT TO:

13. EXT. THE TENNIS COURT AT STONE LODGE
DENZIL drops the tennis racket and makes a grab for SANDY, who shrieks and pretends to push him away. His greater weight forces them slowly to the grass where he begins to undress her with rough urgency, assisted by SANDY. Her blouse buttons spin off. She is bra-less. He buries his face in her breasts while his hand easily probes the waistband of a small Lycra skirt.

> DENZIL
> *Oh, yes, Sandy. Oh yes, oh yes, oh yes.*

67

The afternoon traffic was beginning to build with the mothers in Volvo estates, or neat little sporty jobs joining flexi-time workers – and the giant juggernauts coming away from the motorway to blunder through the drovers' lanes. Once off the main road they were able to walk side by side, conduct a conversation, even. When a car did approach them, its driver stared at the two tall, dark-suited, figures.

'We must look like sodding Mormons,' Denzil said.

'More like bouncers, after a heavy night.'

Ben wiped his bruised mouth with the back of his hand – found it mercifully blood-free.

It has to be now, he thought. Find some words and get them out, now. Another bend and they'd come across the house and estimate how many bungalows could be squeezed into its garden, since the residential home had closed... and why Father hadn't sold to a developer when he'd had the chance. 'I can't imagine what this must feel like,' Ben said.

'It's just how people always say. Can't believe it – won't believe it, you know. I think if Huw was here, it'd be different but... I don't know what I'm going to tell him.'

'It's the suddenness – I guess. You didn't have time. Emma was...'

'She walked in, Ben. She walked in just as normal... still had her coat on. Do you know what she said?'

'No,' Ben said, 'what did she say?'

'She said, "I think it's going to be really warm. The air is all..." and then she just stopped – and she put her hand up to her head and she sat down. And I said "Are you OK?" But she didn't say anything – just looked at me. So I sat next to her – and I put my arms round her – and I was still thinking she'd just... remembered something, you know? Something

68

important that had interrupted her... train of thought. As you can do.'

'Yes.'

'And I put my arms around her... I was sitting there with my arms around her and... that was it. She closed her eyes and, we sort of lay back on the couch... and that was it. I don't mean she was dead – then. She was still alive when the ambulance came... but, that was it you know? "The air is all..." and that was it.'

Denzil had kept walking, accelerating in his agitation. Stone Lodge was there.

The rose garden had been concreted over. Ragwort filled Mother's herbaceous borders, reprising the chapel grounds. The sandstone-block facade had been painted white at some time in the past, the nine sash window frames black – all peeling now.

'It's a tip, isn't it? I don't drive past if I can help.'

'Yeah, a tip,' Ben agreed. 'What's that noise?'

'Just the road – it never stops now. That's why we're all double glazed...'

'No – that other noise... like... a hunt?'

Denzil listened, tuning in, laughed for the first time as his brain brought up the mad, phraseless yelling. 'Boarding kennels. The Lawsons' place down the bottom? It's a kennels now.'

'It used to be so quiet.'

It had been silent that day. His regulation school shoes had slapped the paving at each heavy two-footed landing over cracks. The water butt had resounded to his passing fists. He'd rioted through the heat-dazed garden like an eleven-year-old williwaw and stopped so close to the pair of lovers that he'd caught (but not made out – would never be able to make out, now) Denzil's whispering in the woman's ear. 'Oyster, oyster,' his brother seemed to say.

And he'd stood and watched their white bodies against the dark green leaves and slowly backed away.

'It used to be...' Ben began but he saw that – very slowly – Denzil was sinking to his knees – and then when his knees touched the gravel in front of the gate he let his own bulk carry him forward until his face touched the cool stone of the gatepost, the one unchanged feature of their old home. Deeply and then explosively Denzil began to cry. He knelt beside him, though his joints complained. Denzil's head was tucked well in, defensively turned away. There was nothing to be done.

'We're living on a fucking ice flow, Ben. That's how it feels.'

He'd intended to sleep or at least doze on the train but because he longed for an hour or so's time out from his depression, sleep wouldn't oblige. To think of his brother's life before the happenings of the week had filled him with a settled response of miserable vexation. His sister-in-law's death, he found, had left the feelings hardly worsened at all – no, if he probed around he thought he could just detect a lightening of the misery element. Yes, it definitely felt less... hopeless.

You could never tell, could you?

The loss of a character – even a fully-rounded, vivid, well-established character – could just shift the balance of the piece. The focus moved elsewhere. The narrative gathered pace...

...and let's be honest, he'd never liked Sandy. She had never quite worked for him. No one could witness the dull, underwritten progress of Denzil's existence and not feel it.

When they reached Banbury a beautiful, dark-haired woman in a blue suit came aboard. She settled into the facing seat, the table between them injecting a spurious intimacy to their configuration. She smiled a distant formal smile... with just a hint of alarm or distaste at the cut lip? Huge, hazel eyes turned to the window.

There would be no speech.

She reminded him, pleasurably, of Emma – was more perfectly beautiful than Emma, in fact, though in her late thirties or early forties, older. Almost he reached for the phone to report on his progress but was reluctant to commit the boorish act – and a woman of her age might consider it boorish. Instead he contented himself with opening the small box that sat with his *Independent* and raincoat on the vacant seat. There, in its nest of tissue, lay a silver and enamel snake bracelet, bought on impulse as he wandered around the Graigfawr High Street, waiting for the London train. It was finely modelled, heavy – a real quality item from the turn of the last century. Uncle Tom and a couple of others would've taken their profit on it already, he guessed, before it fetched up in the window of *Bygones*.

He turned it so its marcasite eyes flashed for him. Examined more at leisure, it was a sinister little beast. Not Lalique or even Fouquet, more likely an English creator... Charles Ashbee, perhaps. Emma would know. Emma would love it wrapped around her upper arm.

27. *INT. A RAILWAY CARRIAGE ON THE LONDON TRAIN – NIGHT*
BEN glances over to the beautiful forty-something WOMAN that sits across from him. Very deliberately, holding her gaze, he

takes out a small card box and lays it on the surface between them.

> BEN
>
> *Now how do I know you'll want this?*

> CUT TO:

CLOSE-UP of the WOMAN's face. It remains impassive until very slowly she licks her lips.

> CUT TO:

CLOSE-UP of BEN's fingers tapping the box lid. The WOMAN's hand reaches into shot.

> BEN
>
> *(smiling indulgently)*
>
> *Ah, not so fast! Everything comes to she who waits. Why don't we play a little game...?*

Believing it impossible, he fell asleep and stirred as the brakes took hold at some unidentified spot in the darkness. He woke, as he so often did, *knowing* London was near. As he checked his inside pockets for wallet, ticket and keys his companion risked another smile... less distant, teasing almost, safe in the assurance that soon they'd be parted. She bent forward to retrieve her bag, a white breast half-revealed by the gape of the silk shirt....

He had dreamed – but not about her. In his dream the sun beat fiercely down on the garden of Stone Lodge, a Stone Lodge changed in subtle ways: by his recent visit, most obviously, since huge clumps of ragwort with umbracula the size of sunflowers were occupying the vegetable patch, the vine-house, even the herb-squares set into the terrace.

The water butt he drummed on was painted black but peeling.

Denzil and Sandy writhed, naked, on the tennis court, gleaming and serpentine – literally so. They were legless. Below the waist their bodies tapered to long pale coils – twisted, intertwined, the pulpy stuff of them threshing the cut grass. Horribly flexible, fascinating – they might've been drawn by Blake.

'Bye, now!'

The Beautifully Blue Suited One had just dismissed him.

Stepping down into the clamour of Euston, he looked for Emma even though he knew she couldn't possibly be waiting, wouldn't ever consider meeting him even if he'd made the call.... Sandy and Denzil were falling away, the image of them was dissolving as he sprinted – pushing and pushed by his fellow travellers – up to the taxi rank, out to the real world. His last thought of them as he gave and repeated the Goswell Road address was that it had been so silent, so completely silent that July day... until he'd barged through the heat, clattering and whooping and knocking against any object in range – and they'd heard not a thing.

Oh... and that the girls before Emma and then Emma (and the girls and the women as well as Emma) had never once in his entire life held *him* spellbound – focused in love or lust – unaware of all the rest.

The Ant Garden

It went very quiet after I said what I said.

Llew's *face*.

You know how you stop seeing someone you've lived with for years? How if you were put on the spot and had to describe them – for identification purposes, say – you'd really struggle? That was me. I looked at him (to be honest everybody else was looking in my direction after I said – what I said) and I saw an old man. All of a sudden. I mean, I'd noticed the grey hair and its thinning, like two big bites taken out of his scalp. And you couldn't miss the tramlines across his forehead but he'd had them since his twenties when we first married. (*Look at you*, I remember saying, *you'd think you had the UN to run*). What I hadn't seen before was this sort of falling away of one cheek (down the left side, it was) from beneath the eye to the jaw-line. In fact on that side there was no jaw-line. The extra flesh had settled, all dry and crêpy, along his shirt-collar – and it was putty-coloured against his whites. For a second it all came right again as he swallowed hard and his lips nearly disappeared, but of course he had to let it go, let out his breath and flop – down it dropped. Half a face.

You go through the years with this picture in your mind of the thin, slightly beaky man you've married and just like that it goes fuzzy on you.

'Oh, *Moira!*'

Trisha Pike, I think that was. I'd been meaning all night to tell her the hem was down at the back of that stripy dress she wears for these do's. It's a big room now, the Cornwallis Room (doubled the size with all that cash off the Millennium Fund) but apart from the girls washing up behind the bar, there wasn't a sound. If anyone had moved you'd have heard the new floor creak.

I have to admit I'd come out with a bit more than I meant to (Trisha, Liz Pugh and all that Friends of Theatr Clwyd crowd had got a right earful) but I can't pretend I'm sorry either. It might've been embarrassing at the time but some good came of it. I didn't push so hard for Llew to get his early retirement from the Environmental Health, only to have the likes of Nev Smith and Howie Lloyd round the house whenever they felt like, feet up on the gas-fire surround (both divorced, see, and I wonder why that is?). Or spend Sunday afternoons cutting sandwiches with Trisha Pike in some old pavilion smelling of wet socks – oh, no.

Not me.

It had to be said.

We drove home in silence, over the bridge, up past Shire Hall, where Llew'd worked all those years, in darkness now. Top of the hill the lights were just on the change – but he put his foot down. Straight through we went – nearly hit a cat coming out of the garden of that empty cottage on the corner. Not like him. When we turned off by The Rose and Crown, he only goes and clips the curb. 'I thought you'd been on shandies all night,' I said.

'Dry ginger.'

So after he resigns from the cricket club he proposes to take up painting – and I don't mean the bathroom ceiling, which certainly needed it.

Llew – a painter?

'Who d'you think you are?' I asked him, 'Pedro Picasso? Augustus John? I'll have to run you up a cloak! Anyway, you've left it a bit late.'

Nothing to add, as usual.

That's always been Llew's problem. I think it's why he never got to the upper echelons within the local authority – can't get a point across. You see, the most important aspect of Environmental Health has got to be how you relate to people. I can do it and I've never had his training. But it stands to reason, nobody wants to go giving half the town the trots if only they knew how to avoid it. Bad for business. That was where Llew should've come in. That was Llew's job. He only had to explain things better. And with a bit more force. Then there wouldn't have been all that trouble over the turkeys, Christmas, 2002. Not that I couldn't see it coming. I used to have a joke with our Christine, you know of an evening, when she was off out with her friends: *don't go getting a burger anywhere your father's inspected*!

Well, I'm not one to get in somebody's way. Even though I had two birthday presents to find, market day I go into Mold and while I'm there I buy him the proper paper (something

77

called 'Montval Acid-Free' – which far from being free was expensive) and brushes – a big one for sky and a little one for doing leaves and people and the odd sheep, that sort of thing – and a box of Windsor and Newton water-colours. They're *the real thing*, it says on the lid, *for the amateur and professional*. There's a picture on the front of the box – well it's faded but you can still see it's this nice-looking, elderly gentleman in the corner of a field with his easel up. The woman in Kool Krafts lets me have them for twenty per cent off because of how the Ivory White is missing.

'Oh,' he says when I get it all back – and I'm still trying to thaw out because the ten-to-three is half an hour late – 'that's very nice of you – but you shouldn't have. They've got everything you need down at the Community Centre or they'll let you have it really cheap.'

He could see I wasn't pleased. 'What I'll do,' he says, 'is keep this really good stuff until... I've had the first course of lessons. Pity to waste it till then, eh?'

'Lessons?' I ask.

'With Ray Williams. You remember Ray Williams – used to be the art teacher at Hawarden High? He always did exhibitions at the Oriel Gallery in the summer?' Oh I remembered Ray Williams. Sent our Christine home from school once for something and nothing. I had the headmaster on him. 'He's got his own studio, now. Like a – a proper artist. He gives classes Tuesday afternoons, two till four. Free for the retired...'

'Tuesdays?'

'Two till...'

'*Tuesdays?*' I've had forty years of this sort of thing and still I could hardly believe my ears. 'Tuesdays Christine comes with the kiddies.'

'Yes. Yes, of course she does. Slipped my mind,' he says too quickly, if you ask me.

'What sort of man?' I ask, 'would go out for hours on end when his own daughter and grandchildren were on a visit? And just to sit with a load of other old has-beens, all daubing away like the Brooke Bond chimps?'

'I told you,' he said fooling nobody, 'I just forgot.'

This'll make you laugh. He must've had a go anyway, on his own when I wasn't about. I found them. I was after a dab of white spirit for something or other and there they were – a whole sheaf of crinkled papers in a folder, top shelf, in the garage. They were pathetic for a grown man. Embarrassing. Our little Janey could do better. (She brought home a lovely portrait of me only the other day – 'My Grandma' – with proper legs and arms on, my brown curly hair – which *was* right, once upon a time – and you could even make out my glasses. And she'd let the paint dry properly before putting more to it). But these things – well, for a start they weren't *of* anything – or nothing that I could fathom. He hadn't even bothered to use a pencil – you know, to draw the outlines before he started filling them in? One looked as though it might have been The Great Orme but it had this huge shape hovering over it – just like a blob of Colman's or a flying saucer – with the paint bleeding into what could've been water or sky or the mud flats of Flint for all you could make out. Every one the same, just shades of this with a touch of that – orange, yellow, flaming red. All hot colours.

I gave them to the kiddies to scribble on. If he missed them he never let on – and when it was wet one day I said, 'I think I'll get out those old paints of yours, for the girls,' and he said, 'Might as well.'

It was all quiet after this, for a while. Maybe because Buster went – at last! Thank the Lord, if you ask me. I never found him a very affectionate animal. Always looked at me sideways. It was a big mistake letting him indoors in the first place. Llew again. A good house dog? Don't make me laugh. Any burglars that got in, he'd have been all over them. He'd have fetched the stuff they'd come for, saved them the bother. The way we were going on, that final couple of weeks, I said it was the back of the shed for Buster's box or we'd be having to bite the bullet and go for a new utility floor. Tiles or no tiles, I wasn't going to feel the same about them. Losing it with his bladder, see? Two puddles one night, one huge one the next. And what about my Environmental Health? Never thinks of that. The vet agreed with me, as it happens – we *could've* gone on for years with the dog but there were no guarantees he'd be a hundred per cent trustworthy again. And there was our Christine's girls. What am I expected to do, bar them from the house? We've got the utility child-proofed, of course, but accidents happen. And if one of them had got in there somehow, sometime and put their little hands down where that's been? Anyway the vet takes Buster off in a bag and Llew's moping around as though we'd lost a close relation. No excuse, see, to disappear for half an hour or more, morning, afternoon and night. Him and Buster would be hanging around on the edge of the rugby pitch watching practice, or Llew'd be getting talking to those old misery-guts fishing the Alyn. I said to Christine, 'Don't be surprised to see him in a black armband.' We did laugh. But then she came back with something that really wiped the smile off my face. 'Just be careful, Mum – he's at that funny age where men go electronic.'

'What d'you mean?' I said.

'Oh, they buy complete new music systems and start collecting Sounds Of The Seventies CD's. They send for them out of the colour-sup...or they can download them, that's what they're doing now. They get a computer and they surf the Net and sit up till the early hours, talking to some woman called Candy from Pasadena.'

'How?'

'Chat rooms, e-mails! God, Mother, where've you been? E-mails! Lawrence gets them at work all the time.'

'From women?' I said.

'No,' she said, 'from people ordering plastic windows and replacement doors.'

Anyway I was that concerned about this music and computing mania – it got so I'd cross the road rather than walk past Dixons – I missed what he was really up to at first.

Yoghurt cartons on the windowsill, that's how it started. Yoghurt cartons full of leaf-mould and some little thing he'd dug up out of the woods. I just threw the lot away with the peelings. I'd see him looking for them, on the quiet you know, but we didn't mention it.

Then, one afternoon, a Wednesday it'd be, he finds me in the market. I was just talking to Liz, who's got her niece Gaynor's new baby with her and she's telling us all about the terrible vomiting problem the child's had since, well, really ever since it came out of hospital – been as far as Liverpool with it, Gaynor has, seeing specialists. And you'd never have thought it because it's a beautiful baby with a shock of dark hair, nothing like Gaynor or her husband I *had* to say. Anyway I turn to go and Llew has slipped off. When he comes back, he's got this bedraggled thing in a pot under one arm.

Crataegus-something-or-other. It's just a hawthorn like you get in the hedges. But he's paid for it, of course, like a mug.

I say my piece about 'whatever will Liz think' and then, 'That's a poor specimen,' I point out.

'Yes, Moira,' he says, 'that's why I bought it.'

So it began. Before the week's out the straggly plant is in its own special saucer, roots draped over a bit of sandstone, its branches – such as they are – wrapped in fuse wire and then bent out at odd angles. The wire makes them stick that way, apparently.

'Looks like a lavatory brush,' I tell him.

'It's bonsai. The Japanese art of growing miniature trees. I'm just going for 'hokidachi' at first,' he says, as though I'm interested. 'Broom style, that means. It seems like the simplest form – for a complete beginner.'

That's when I see he's clutching this little book, *Introducing Bonsai*.

'And how much was that?' I ask.

'Twenty pence. The library was selling it off. Nobody's taken it out for years.'

'I'm not surprised,' I said.

It's not long before the hawthorn is joined by every variety of twiggy stuff. There's a juniper, a cypress, another sort of thorn, a pyracantha, a larch – in fact a whole group of larch. He has them arranged in order of height so that from one side they became a tiny wood – or a proper, full-sized wood, seen from a long way off. Even I had to admit it was almost clever. I say 'had' because Janey and Jade got this real passion for tennis soon after and the larch-wood was one they broke.

I watched him sweep it up. It was in a flat green dish and he picked the pieces up a bit at a time and held them there, just staring. Surely it couldn't be that he was planning to put them back together? Any fool could see it was the sort of breakage that wouldn't mend. Still he stared.

You say a single word to those kiddies, I was thinking – but he didn't. One of the little trees he must've been able to save. It goes into a square yellow pot all on its own, only now it's got a weight hanging off it and it's near doubled-up. No longer 'Yose-Ue', it's now 'Han-kengai' or semi-cascade style, he tells me when he catches me looking.

'Sounds like a disease,' I say. 'Hang-ken-gooy. 'Praps that's what you've got.'

Well there must be some explanation – something that can make sense of a sixty-year-old who will spend an hour (I know because I've timed him) *an hour* collecting up the fallen berries from under a twelve-inch high cotoneaster that's meant to look like an apple tree – and then arranging them in heaps of five and seven under its pigmy little branches.

'What for?' I said.

'So that it looks as though someone has been picking the fruit and has it all ready – to go into boxes, say.'

'Who's been picking it? An ant?'

'No,' he says, 'not an ant,' and he sighs – as though I'm the stupid one. And off he goes. It's freezing cold, nearly dark, but there's Llew back and forward, primping up the moss round this one with a special tool, feeding another.

Would you credit it? He actually gives them names?

He names the trees – and they say poor Prince Charles has lost the plot.

There's 'Stork Ascending' and 'Maple Palm' – and more.

I asked him why – why the names? I mean, does he need to address the thing personally before he sets about it with the nail-scissors? What do you say to a small tree in a pot when you're lopping off all the new growth it's struggled to produce through the year?

'Don't worry, Maple Palm, this might sting a little.'

'I'm sorry Stork Ascending – this is going to hurt me more than it hurts you.'

He doesn't answer, of course – just smiles, shakes his head.

Occasionally I might get a 'very witty, love'. And he carries on: pruning, titivating, wiring this bit up and this bit down, rubbing off the fresh buds with a fingernail. Watering with cold, weak tea. Standing back to admire. It gives me the creeps to watch.

One day, when he'd been out there all afternoon and I was waiting to go into town, I stormed onto the patio – that's where he keeps them on their special wooden racks.

'Have you any idea,' I said, 'how much time you waste on these things? I mean it's not as if it's proper gardening. I do the garden – like always. A right mess you made of it when you had a go.'

He straightened up. It's close work. He's had to put his reading-glasses on and was paring away at the bark of this stunted conifer in its turquoise pot – really going at it, with a wicked looking scalpel, can you believe? And he must've found it pretty absorbing because his face, that one side of his face, I mean, had loosened until it was well-nigh onto his chest.

'You look just like Dr Mengele,' I said, 'you know, that old Nazi? What on earth are you doing? You'll kill it.'

'It's called sharimiki,' he told me, staring at me but not really able to focus. I have the same problem these days. I knew I was just a big, dark-coated blur to him. 'Sharimiki. It means 'driftwood-style'. You shave the outer-layers of xylem off – very precisely, very gradually – over a long, long period... so... so that in the end it seems as though the tree has withstood years and years of battering.'

He held it up as though I was expected to admire his handiwork. All I could see was some sort of pathetic, ravaged Scots Pine affair. Its crown is a congested mass of dark green needles, like a witches broom. The little twisted trunk's only part the proper cinnamon colour – the rest's bone-white where it's been scraped back by the blade.

'You want to mind yourself with that thing.'

Takes no notice, does he?

'I'm going to call this one 'On The Edge'. D'you see? It's stood there and taken the worst life can throw at it... it's twisted and writhed as every season got worse... the summers, one long drought, the winters nothing but snow and ice and blizzard... it's been starved of warmth and light, kept short of everything it might have needed to grow... and it's still there, alive, just about. Hanging on.'

Treeline

That was the thing to keep in mind: none of it was George's fault.

'I'm sorry Reverend,' said the little man who had been nipping in and out of the low doorway for the past hour, rehearsing and anticipating this moment. 'I'm sorry,' he repeated, 'she won't come down. I thought she would – I was sure I could get her to this morning, you know, when... you know, when I talked to you....'

With an effort the Reverend (who, in old denims and washed-out T-shirt, looked more like one of the dirty-nail caste than the farmer he'd come to see) wrenched his eyes away from the middle distance. A newish barrow was blocking out what had been a fine view up the valley. Beyond though, still beautiful, still desirable, reared Moel Ferch – Daughter of Hills. It was approaching noon and her fawn top was touched by the high sun, her flanks tinted by some absent artist with a bottle-green smudge of plantations.

He focused, instead, on the gabbling figure.

'I've been here a few years now, George. I think you might call me Matthew.'

The smaller, older man couldn't respond to the proposition. He dismissed it as he had once discounted some uneconomic offer on the season's lambs. It didn't work – it made no sense – therefore it mustn't have been made at all. 'Any-road,' he ran on, 'I thought she might just come down for you... knowing you were coming... you, especially... on account of being so good – really good when *it* happened... you know....'

Something else to keep in mind about George Davies – you just had to let him wind down.

The end of speech seemed to release the dog, poised between them. It yawned, stretched the forelegs, stretched a spine discernable beneath the black and grey pelt and wandered in a slow arc to a position behind Matthew's legs; Matthew's shoes were well sniffed – though they can have smelt of nothing but the thin khaki slime in which both men and dog stood.

'Gerr-outta it, Ty!'

The small man's sudden harshness had Matthew blinking, the collie slinking off.

'It's all right George. Really... em, look. It's a pity Enid doesn't feel she can see me. Give me a call – anytime. Today, even, later today if you think – if she changes her mind. I should be home after six... if she does change her mind.'

George's anger or humiliation must have had a pungency far stronger than the soupy surface of the yard. It forced Ty into an even lower, defensive posture. Crawling towards a door-less, purposeless, wooden structure that leaned against the house wall, the collie scrambled over an accretion of baler-twine bits, black polythene, blue polythene and broken, old hay-bales. Here emerald grass sprouted like cress. His master turned away. 'Can't see it, Reverend.'

And then, as though the dog's demeanour had suggested itself to his own wiry frame, his shoulders slumped. 'If she don't do something soon, we're gonna have to have the nurse in... she's getting sore heels... all that lying, you know... I just wish....'

'I know.'

Matthew slewed the aged Metro (pursued by a second truant collie, snapping at its wheels) left at the Davies' gate... firmly left – down the hill, down towards the village, away from Moel Ferch. The animal peeled off only when he drew level with the final bit of Davies land; just inside the gate you could catch a glimpse of the still-bare patch where fire had baked the acid ground – a black O, like the entrance to a pit from above... from up there... where he was *not* going... not today.

Now who said virtue was its own reward? Having made the decision, he found he was trapped behind a quarry wagon carrying just three improbably huge boulders. Perhaps it was the enforced lack of pace that had him noticing the houses down this, the tattiest approach to the village. Just before the bend were a row of grey semis. Their peeling eau-de-nil paint and shaggy gardens suggested ownership by some public body: council, water company, forestry. In fact he knew they'd been put up for the quarrymen. At the first he pulled to a halt and braved the squelch of lawn and the brilliant children's playthings to approach the front door. From within, a baby wailed. By the Doppler effect Matthew could chart its progress as it was carried along the hall.

'Hello, Kathy,' he said to the baby-carrier, 'I've just been up to the Farm.'

'Oh, yes?' The girl's narrowed eyes and pursed lips told their own story.

'I'm Matthew Humphries. From the church?'

'Oh, yeah.' She shifted the weight of the still-screaming child to the opposite hip where she gave it a none-too-tender bounce.

'Getting big,' Matthew almost hollered.

'Yeah, well, Roy don't believe in christening.'

'I didn't mean that – it's, er, your mother. Your father thought she might just get up... thought I might be able to talk to her. But, no.' He shook his head.

'No, it's a funny thing, depression. I had it terrible after this one. Nothing they give me did any good.'

Bounce, bounce went the baby.

'It's been months though.'

'Yes, well, it's Dad I feel sorry for. When we had the sheep – all those years we had the sheep – Mum did nothing but gripe about 'em. Then they have to go – well everybody was in the same boat, everybody lost their animals – but now we get all this...' Matthew watched her bite back the expletive for his benefit, 'all this blasted nonsense. I know it's not so much the foot-and-mouth as... the other thing. What Dad did. But you can't blame him – not really.' She wiped a free hand down her side and onto a bare inch of midriff. The temperature was soaring... the air was dense with moisture... the child's plump legs sticking, skin on skin. 'But they've had the money through. The compo. Up to them, isn't it? Re-stock or pack it in. Up to them. 'Course Dad can't make his mind up to do anything, not with her stuck in bed like some... invalid.'

'As you say, though, it's a funny thing – depression. Makes you do funny things.'

Bounce, bounce, bounce went the baby causing it to nod in agreement.

He had a handful of others to see... worthy visits: now, towards the week's end they had begun to squeeze and pinch like the books forced into too little space along his study shelves... and, just as with the books, came the urge to leave them to their discomfort...

...there was Mac at The Pair of Pigeons. He had closed the back room – this was the back room where, for a few seasons, a resentful wife had served all the local specialities: Thai Scampi, Lancashire Hotpot and Mississippi Mud Pie. This was the wife that had gone home to Chester and taken the kids. Mac was offering some old stacking chairs for the Young Families' Club... or at least for the two young families who'd so far made use of it... and who were never to be joined by Kathy and her large irritable baby (the name and sex of which he hadn't known because the surly and absent Roy didn't believe in christening)... no, not red-eyed Mac... instead he turned the car around, finding the breath coming easier, the blood returning to the clenched hands, now that he'd given in to it.

Today, he could not come down.

The lane, if you kept to the left fork, skirted the Davies' farm to the south and wandered through a wide clearing of pounded hardcore where the forestry vehicles turned. Then it dived into his favourite piece of planting: Moel Ferch's skirts of larch wood. There was a scrub-willow thicket along the edge, sprung up before the conifers had really got going and into this he could inch the Metro, carefully, very carefully feeling at every revolution of the front wheels for that lurch of soft earth... until the silver grey leaves covered the windscreen. The car became invisible. From here it was all footwork.

A deer-track took him along a limestone ridge, dipped to avoid a pool-cum-bog where water forget-me-nots still bloomed and then shot straight upward in a calf-cramping climb of half a mile. The ascent was a firebreak now high with coarse grasses and campions and faded foxgloves... and heat. This was not an enjoyable section and with the sun on his back and the midges settling on bare damp arms, it offered little in return for the effort... and yet... and yet, it was part of it, a necessary element in the endeavour. To get that worst bit over with – and through it to push the mind and the heart ahead of the protesting legs, knowing how he was about to feel, sure of what he was going to think, that was the trick. That was something to relish.

Larch... someone had once told him that if you must have trees ('and you must because the soil is good for damn all else') and if you must have conifers ('and you must because they take the warmth and wet and make planks out of it quicker than anything native') larch, though alien, makes the most beautiful woods. Less grasping and greedy than your fir or your spruce, it shares the sunlight for half a year with the ground it grows in, puts on needles and returns them, courteous as a rowan. Here at the top of the useless and overgrown firebreak the larches were tall and clean-limbed as telegraph poles with the odd graceful curve of a ferny arm reaching forty feet above his head. He leant with his back against one old giant, closed his eyes on the bright phantom spots in his vision and waited. His destination, the thing he was after, it was still a good fifteen minutes away. Once the pulse in his ears had dimmed the quiet seeped through him like brandy. To shatter it, 'I'm Matthew Humphries – from the church!' he shouted to startled blackbirds and circling crows. 'That's the church. That's the little grey job – next to The Spar!'

Somewhere out of sight a dull boom began, bounced off the sides of the hidden valley and came back at him through the trees. Once, he supposed, the sort of man that he was would've felt answered... would've cowered, perhaps – but at least cowered in the certain knowledge that someone, or something, had noticed him... it was really just like old George Davies down there. No one could really blame him – not for killing and burning his wife's pet goats – a useless sacrifice (as it turned out) to the Plague God. He had put the gun to the silky white heads while Enid begged and wept – and finally cursed him. But George had shot the nannies and their bleating kids, small and impractical as toys – all in the pitiable mis-belief that anything any of them did could make a difference.... A thousand years from now would some delving scholar speculate about the dark religious mysteries enacted in the Davies' fields? First, the offering of goats on their lesser pyre – and then the great mound of ewes, slaughtered, burned and thatched over with the land that had bred them.

Would the scholar wonder if a priest were present at these cruellest of rites?

The trees were changing now. He made his way up the last, almost gentle slope. Only sitkas, hated by foresters for their fearsome armoury of spines, could hang on up here. He walked in the narrow way, careful to keep bare arms out of their grasp, careful in stumbling never to reach out to their metallic spikes for balance or support. The precise grid of their planting gave no expectation of chance vistas but led with a firmness that lifted his heart to his secret goal.

The cottage.

Built for a shepherd when the bricks for his church were still clay, it had been caught by the rising tide of trees – not demolished but planted up to and around; its roof gone, its beams rotted, the alien spruce had pinched its walls to final collapse... but their victory was partial. Here the forest itself failed. Sit on the stone cairn of the cottage front wall and the only thing left above you was Moel Ferch's smooth, pale pate. Look down, over the heads of the trees, and the Davies' farm drowsed, empty and green with its black spot and Enid watching it from her narrow retreat. Beyond that the model of a village had been laid out beside a bit of a river: a row of cottages, a Victorian villa, an enclave of bungalows... a four by four slid out of The Pair of Pigeons' car-park, a delivery-van manoeuvred in front of the Spar. For a minute or maybe many minutes, nothing stirred at all and then a quarry wagon crept through his field of vision, past the church, past the Cross with its bus stop and War Memorial... speeding up as it turned onto the coast road with three more giant rocks.

Everything was so small, so inconsequential from here – *so far down*.

Boom came the quarry's retort.

He felt it this time before he heard it: a *basso profundo* rumble that began at his feet and seemed to force its way out through the top of his skull.

But no need to cower, no need beg for aid or assistance – easy to understand that on Enid's painted bedside chest, the glass of water stirred... and that at his back – just beyond the horizon, Roy, who didn't hold with christening, was blasting free a little more of Moel Ferch, Daughter of Hills, ready for carting away.

Free Again

Free again. That was how to think of it. *Free again, Teg.* That was how his Mum had put it with her eyes narrowed and her lips nothing but a line of red. A nasty way with words, his Mum had, even when they were blameless bits of sound on their own. You could rely on Mum to put an edge on.

Or well-rid. There was another phrase. Inchy – or was it Glyn? one of them anyway – had said that in The Brewers' only last night.

Well rid of her, mate.

'Course nobody'd say it to your face, not when you and her were still... you know, rubbin' rudies. But we didn't have a lot of time for her. Nobody round here did. Just taking you for a ride – anyone could see it.

(That would've been Inchy. Always the mouthy one, Inchy. Always with more to say for himself than he had to say).

This Saturday, fuck this place! We'll go right over to Liverpool. Night on the fucking town, a proper fucking town! Night out in scally-land. Back clubbing it, that's what'll do it for you. Plenty more fish in the Mersey.

He was walking along Wood Street, he thought, though Wood Street not as bright and on the boil as it should've been. But there was still illumination to see Wood Street by. It was all slick as though it had rained, shiny... though where the light was coming from... it must be coming *out* of somewhere, stood to reason out from somewhere – but *no*. All the doorways and panes of glass – high up only, these, well above the doorways, you could see the sense in it, though – and shutters, *every second fuckin' one with shutters*, and all dark. Nothing leaking out from any of them, nowhere behind any of them where Inchy and Glyn and those girls – two girls – might still be. It was like Wood Street had been turned right round and all the stuff that had made up Wood Street was pointing somewhere else. This, that he'd wandered into, this must be Wood Street's arsehole... and that stink, that rotting stink, was Wood Street's fart.

A Wood Street fart, someone said.

Too fuckin' true, he answered – but in doing it he fell against a metal grill that sounded off and must've frightened them away.

When the grill quietened he looked up at the sky. It was black and low, a black curved temporary roof over Wood Street, if it was Wood Street... Inchy saying in his best voice *We've just plastic-ed it up for the time being, love. (Ninety quid for now – just materials). Keep out the rain, that will, till we can get back and do it proper for you.*

Plastic-ed it up. Nobody but Inchy said plastic-ed it up.

Oh, right. Thanks. And when d'you think...?

Yeah, no worries. That'll keep you all all right. Bye now. Give you a ring, yeah?

When you gonna do that, Inchy?

When Wrexham wins the Champions League!

A while ago there'd been these two girls – big girls, both of them, tall as himself which put them towering over Inchy. One was a dark-haired girl that smelled wonderful, hot and sweet with a juicy mouth tasting of fruit, but some fruit he didn't know. The moist round arms on her made him hot and sad at the same time because her arms felt just like *her* arms, out of the shower, slippery and smooth as leather belts up the inside, like two belts whipping around his body and tangling themselves behind his back. Pincher-fingers, dipping into him, sending shock waves up and down his spine, hurtful and sweet with it... the other girl was....

He couldn't see the other girl. Couldn't see her face, couldn't even remember if she was dark or blonde – but tall, she was tall. *Looked a fuckin' scream with Inchy, Inchy having to stretch it out just to get a snog up against that window.*

Don't mind him, Inchy saying to somebody he can't quite make out – but dark haired, she has dark hair just like....

Don't mind old smacked-arse face, love. In mourning he is, see? What? Death of his sex-life! Passed away it did, quietly in its sleep. RIP!

Give it a rest, Inchy, Glyn saying.

What? Give what a rest?

You know leave him – just cut the bollocks, eh?

This is my main man, this is. This is Glyn what's calling me a bollocks. Him?

What you want to know his name for? Unless you got another mate. Anyway, can't tell you his name, can I? You'll only go and piss yourself laughing.

At the end of Wood Street the area would open out into a wide paved rectangle with a precinct, shops and seats in the middle of it all because cars weren't let in. How he knew this, as an infrequent visitor to the city, he failed to wonder. The picture of paving, seats and beyond a blue and white sign were clearer than anything else in his mind – clearer, say, than what exactly his arms were doing as he progressed from one silent, shuttered frontage to the next. Paving, seats, sign saying CAR PARK in white on blue though if he squeezed his eyes tighter shut than tight shut, it became blue on white. A negative. It's where he should make for. He was being urged to do this by something that appeared to be outside himself.

Whatever or whoever it is doing the urging, it has so far kept back from the slopping wave of drink that has weighted his legs, that has filled his boots and threatens to surged tidally through his head at every eye-movement... look down and a bit to the front, that was it. Look at some line that you pretended was there and follow it straight until – any minute now – there'd be paving stones, square grey stones under your feet and then there'd be those benches you'd clocked on the walk here and you could sit on one of them and no – go past them and the sign would say – in blue and white it'd say...

Without warning the ground dissolved and he was jolted forward. A fall of only a few inches... a curb he understood that now, he'd stepped off a curb but it was enough to swing his body around in a quick half-circle. Sitting down heavily he felt but didn't feel his buttocks strike the road. He waited for it to settle. There was a good quality to the surface, strokably good. Hands ran across it without being told... such a good, cool road. Wood Street – if it was Wood Street? Cool Wood Street? No better street could ever have existed. Although bitty and sore in his palms, it was this that made for friendliness – and an antidote to the soft sloshing that was now everywhere inside him.

A woman giggled.

At the start – just where the giggle began – it was a fine sound, light and clear, reminding him of *her*, how everything could be turned to a joke which he'd never known in a girl before. Breaking things, that could be funny, losing stuff, tripping over... which is what he must have done just now. But this wasn't her giggle. This laugh got deeper and hoarser, got to be less of a laugh the longer it went on... he couldn't see who it was was laughing but before that laugh finished, he'd decided he didn't want to...

They came from behind him, parted to get around. Three or maybe more blokes, just the one woman – Christ she was his Mum's age! Now that was funny. Some footballer... GRAB-A-GRANNY front page... some footballer and a tart...

Doing a Wayne Rooney, lads? Teg suggested.

The first pain came in his hip, just below the joint and worse than an Inchy tackle on a Sunday morning. When he rocked to that side there was another pain that took him in the back and nearly stopped his breath. Weird thing was none of them said a word – not a single sound after that laugh and his own question. And after the question he found himself being completely quiet, knowing somehow that *quiet was it, Teg.* That anything else was real shit...

Pain! and then a double pain where two feet synchronise their contact... a final grunt of effort from one of them that produces real agony in his shoulder but not his head, *that's tucked in, boy, where your fuckin' foot can't find it.* Then it's over. They are walking away. Teg's eyes don't tell him this but the footsteps and just before they fade that giggle, that giggle returns as though this bit with Teg has been no interruption at all, ta la.

Chucking up is back on the agenda now but when he opens his eyes and rolls into position, he finds he can't do it. Lacks the strength. Who would've thought you needed to be fit to chuck up, that you needed to be in training? Should be as easy as throwing the stuff down your neck...

The vomit surges up and out like a cistern emptying. He can't resist the urge to hunch over. *A human U-bend – now that is funny! ... better now, though.*

Stand up.

Teg obeyed. Christ that must've been some tackle of Inchy's. His whole bloody leg felt useless, rubber-boned. Both palms against the wall, and then the top of his head also against the wall between them, he finds he can maintain himself, if not standing up exactly, then not on the ground. After a while and making sure not to depend at any time on that rubber leg, he can swivel so that his back is to the building he has been lying in front of. Progress.

He can call Inchy. Somewhere out there in the darkness is Inchy – and Glyn. But Inchy is the one to call... and in his pocket, by some miracle, is still his phone. Shame is there as he fumbles it out – Inchy'll be a complete wanker over Teg ending up like this, needing a pick-up but he'll come, he and Glyn, with or without those two big girls. But without would be best.

Inchy?

No.

It's Teg.

Go on!

Look... um... where the fuck are you, Inchy? There's a long wait for this to be answered during which that giggle, that woman's giggle, gets into the phone.

Where the fuck are you?

I dunno. Just dunno. I'm... not so good. Coming to get me, are you?

He thought he heard 'not so good' and laughter. An echo. Not the phone's fault. There was someone with Inchy, laughing.

How can I? Inchy's voice continues but too low for Teg to catch it, not meant for Teg, is it? *What can you see? Where you are, what are you looking at?*

Fuck all.

Shit.

That rubber leg is threatening to undo all Teg's good work. He feels it tremble, feels the foot edge out and from under him of its own accord. *I'm fuckin' bleedin', Inchy.* Until he says it, it isn't true. Now it is. *Bleedin' Inchy!* Stuck to his hand with it, the phone is.

Shi-t-te!

The action of sitting down again is almost underway. Teg pushes off from the wall, takes one step and another, the movement keeping him upright. Like a helicopter. *Like a fucking helicopter!*

What? No – forget it. Look Teg, man, you gotta get into a taxi, OK? Get to somewhere busy, with the cabs outside, you know? Get in a cab and get it to take you to... hang on. Glyn!

Glyn! Pier Head, yeah? Did you get that? Get to the Pier Head and we'll have the car there. Yeah? Are you gonna do that, Teg?

OK.

Pier Head, Teg. Ten minutes. Fuckin' do it.

Yeah.

The Pier Head sounds good. He remembers ferries... his Nan, never his Mum, taking him on the boats, the smell of the Mersey under them, the taste of the river hitting you in the face on account of how it was always rough, never summer, never bright and calm not in Liverpool...

When he thinks to put the phone back his fingers close around a crumpled wad of something that's also there: too dark to read it but don't need to read it. It's the back torn off a birthday card – there never being anything like writing paper in the flat it's all she can have found. One side *Happy Birthday, Lover-Boy! From Lover-Girl Lisa*, on the other side what she'd wanted to say – ending in *better off going*.

There'd been some of that before, though – like the time she broke the light in Inchy's car, just messing about she was and broke that little bulb over the mirror and Inchy had a right go at her – always the mouthy one, Inchy – and Teg hadn't said... because – why did she have to go messing about like that in *Inchy*'s car, for fuckssake? So now you can't see inside it to use your phone, check your cash, nothing.

Inchy has promised it, so he expects the busy place, the one with the cabs, to be just at the end of this street, the one he's in. It comes as a shock to find that for once Inchy's wrong – at the end of the street there's another one, just as dark and empty. Bigger buildings though. Look up and – *Jesus no, don't look up!* The pain makes him shout, that pain from his shoulder that without warning had got into his head. Don't look up again, Teg, no cabs up there, forward that's the way for you. Surely *that* was something, though? There you go, not like old Inchy to get it wrong – and the light was flickering which meant traffic – *had to* and all he need do now was get into it and the cab Inchy had sent for him would be there, doors open, waiting to receive him onto its comfy back seat.

One hand checking the wall he blunders along, his eyes aching with the effort of keeping the glare in them when what they really wanted to do was to close right down and let him get along by touch. *Keep on staring into brightness, Teg. Inchy and Inchy's motor are where...* but a thick iron railing has placed itself across his belly. Another is at the level of his thighs. Beyond it, the lights continue their dance but this stupid fuckin' railing is keeping him back. Where's the sense in it?

Anger drives him on, in one wet hand there's the cold of the metal which although an enemy is friendly in the way it keeps him upright, keeps him... *move it Teg, get fuckin' going, will you?*

Come on our Teg, the boat won't wait!

You could always smell the water just before you saw it... always could.

Come on!

He can hear Inchy's voice surely, which only goes to show how Inchy always comes up trumps – how the blackness that he is falling gratefully into now must be the dark of Inchy's car.

Dinner on the Roof

Of course in Wales we'd never known winters like these. Snow I remembered on Moel Ferch four years out of five but this... this was something different. Ten feet of snow could fall in a couple of days – and then a storm might blow up as the finale, bringing what Annie called the ice-rain: a white terror of huge glass–crystals the weight of which could bow down birches and hemlocks, cedars and fir.

Birches and hemlocks cow-towed, graceful as girls but not Captain Cedar: he'd stand there through the short day and then, in the mid-darkness, would crack – a terrible retort, blasting us all awake and setting little Marged screaming till dawn.

The winter of '39 was the worst. Cold and sickness: it killed the ragged ends of families up and down the valley and you could hear the children and old people coughing themselves inside out, trying to get the thick lumps of air back where it belonged. It got into town though the buildings huddled close as wagons and you'd think there'd be protection. It racked John Jones' wife (who had been Annie's bridesmaid) over three days until one night she sat straight up in her bed and cried 'John! John! They've set fire to the store!' and died in his arms. After the funeral Iorwerth said we should stay out of Drum Creek and let the fever pass. I'd lie awake in my bunk up in the cabin eaves and listen to them bicker. My sister's voice, a sweet contralto, had become bitter as the sheepberries that grew along the Albertan streams. 'It's John Jones that has fed us for the last month,' she hissed. I was still a boy but enough of a man to know how Iorwerth would flinch, run his small hands through his fine brown hair, look anywhere but at his wife.

'Without John Jones we'll starve,' Annie moaned and I thought I heard Iorwerth moan too; neither spoke another syllable so that all of us but Marged had the prospect of drifting off with this cheerful thought as the last in our heads.

I'd heard it all from up there: the close words of a married couple that has shared the same past and the same present... the scraps and resentments boiling up from a life of murderous work... and these could be followed by soft, babyish lovemaking that made me wonder what came over a stony man like my brother-in-law. How was it that women did this thing to men, turning them into something unrecognisable even to themselves?

'Without John Jones we'll starve,' Annie had said and the silence that followed kept me restless through the dark hours.

Next morning Iorwerth was up, stoking the stove, heating water to wash us all, which Annie made us do before we ate or drank. Mam and Nain would never be dead while my sister was alive.

I chewed Annie's oatcakes and drank the weak tea and Iorwerth sat apart and oiled his old Lee-Enfield, with its split stock.

'I'll be away then,' he muttered as though this were the end of a long conversation, which it wasn't. Talk is cheap, people say in Wales and wherever they go from Wales. They must be the sort who've never had to price up anything. When food and clothes and kerosene and medicines for a sick child are all out of a family's reach, talk isn't cheap. Every word costs more than the grown-ups can ever hope to spend.

'Sleep out in this and you won't wake up,' Annie told him. 'Don't go.'

'What's in the root store, Bobi?' he said, turning to me.

Now here's a low blow, I thought, bringing me in. They can't look at each other, but they'll both look at me. Even little Marged's huge green eyes were turned my way, knowing something was on the go but as always with Marged never knowing what. She began to gurgle with excitement and to rock back and forth in the rough wooden chair.

'Leave the boy out of it...' Annie started.

'What's in the root store, Bobi?' Iorwerth said.

'Nothing,' I answered him, feeling a traitor to my sister. 'You know. There's nothing in the root store bar a few rotten potatoes. Lift the hatch, you can smell 'em.'

I was so unused to anyone doing anything I said that when Iorwerth dragged up the trap door in the planks, held it for an instant and let it crash down I nearly joined Marged in her wild, infantile applauding... and when she decided the noise had frightened her and started to yell fit to shake the snow off the shingles, I felt like joining in that too.

109

Iorwerth pulled the coat of Welsh wool over everything else he had on. 'I'll be away then,' he said. 'Bobi – you'll look to the ladies.'

And he went. He really did.

Annie wouldn't but I ran out and watched him trudge down the trail and around the bend, the carbine propped over one narrow shoulder, the drifts pulling at the thin legs in John Jones' cast-off boots.

As if to mock us the sun rose by mid-morning, the first sun of the year with any real heat in it. We faced due south. The clearing and the cabin and Iorwerth's empty barn and stock-proof corral dripped twenty carat diamonds into the old white crust. By afternoon it was warm enough for Marged to play with the wooden horse I'd made her out on the porch, and she laughed and chattered like a regular child. You could almost forget that behind the water-ice eyes, there was something frozen and stuck fast in her little head that nothing would ever melt.

Annie beat the rugs and beat the blankets in her female misery and when there was nothing left that could hold wood-ash and dust she turned on me. 'Don't go lounging around all afternoon, Bobi! You're as tall as a man now – you eat as much as a man. Get in here and stir this pot.'

Iorwerth's parting words slipped into my head in time to still the rudeness already on my tongue. 'Show me,' I said, meek as Marged on one of her good days.

It breaks my heart now to think of it: Annie's soup. The ways of doing things that people leave behind them... they can cut you sharper than an old pin in the back of a drawer. In the stewpan, scoured bright as a new coin, was every bit of potato and rutabaga she'd spent the morning cutting off from our rotting store. And there were peppercorns and her last bunch of sage and I could smell the wild garlic that Annie pretended she didn't use and a handful of precious meal to thicken the lot.

'Don't let it catch, *bach*,' she said patting my arm. 'We'll have some when the taters have dropped. I'll go and see what that bad girl of mine is up to.' But she stepped over Marged and the wooden toy, red hands clutching at the sides of her face, her eyes fixed on the trail.

In the pot the bits and pieces gradually lost themselves, became translucent and fell without a struggle into the creamy broth, until only the peppercorns and sage stalks were left. Round and round they went, bobbing down, you thought, for the very last time only to see them reappear. The ladle couldn't grind them against the bottom – oh, too quick for that, they were – but I just had some old leaf pressed up and caught fast on one side when...

'Bobi!' Annie called. Times like this you're meant to be able to recognise that special tone in the voice but I was a boy hypnotised by hunger and steam and soup.

'Bobi!' she called again. 'Come here.'

Two tall figures were walking towards our cabin – not along the trail which had taken away Iorwerth and not back towards town and its ailing folk. They had slid – I could see where from their tracks – straight out of the firs and across the untouched snow. Tall and tawny, they were, with the uniform faces of a pair of brothers.

'Indians!' Annie hissed.

I had never seen Indians. I had never met anyone who had seen Indians – and when asked, Annie and Iorwerth just turned away. We'd been living in their land as long as Marged was old and we'd never met its proprietors.

111

How can I describe them now, after all this time? They were neither sly nor brash – they moved towards us in a way unlike any man or woman or child that was known to me. It put me in mind of a cat crossing its own farmyard and a horse its own pasture – intent as hunters, wary as prey.

They stopped a couple of feet from the porch steps and looked us over. Me first, but quickly, dismissively, murmuring low liquid words that made my cheeks burn. In any language on earth you can catch 'Just a boy' when the boy is you.

Annie next... my beautiful sister that I'd never seen as a woman before, with her heart-shaped face that Iorwerth took between his hands to kiss when they thought I slept. Up the steps toward her they came as though it were all rehearsed and I jumped forwards, frightened of them, but more terrified of being just that boy.

'No, no, Bobi,' Annie said, 'that's good... that's... just hold your place.' And I was so used to obeying her, 'just a boy' did what she said.

Two rifles clattered onto the wet boards as they squatted down next to Marged. Slowly, one of them stroked her head. Everything was fascinating: the roughly-hewn toy with its painted saddle and shoe-lace reins, Marged's nearly-white plaits and her tiny blue boots.

And they held me in their turn. They were men though nowhere near Iorwerth's years. Their old skin jerkins were open to the waist despite the freezing air. Against polished-deal chests necklaces rattled as they moved. We had all been told the stories of how Indians had once been cheated and gulled out of all they owned by the offer of cheap trinkets: shiny beads, brooches of glass... so that it seemed they had no more sense or caution than the magpies, stealing any bit of bright trash. But these necklaces were of huge ivory thorns, wicked as weaponry... and the look of the wearers was shrewd.

'See,' Annie whispered. 'They have bear's teeth around their necks.'

'What does it mean?'

'They must be... Haida, is it? Or Kut-en-ai? I don't know.' She shook her head slowly. 'They're meant to be all gone from here.'

'But what are the bear's teeth for?'

'For? They're not for anything.' Annie's sharp tone had our guests exchanging quizzical glances. 'It means they'll have killed a bear. They... they worship the bears but sometimes – when they've no choice – they have to kill one for food... as Iorwerth killed the pig,' she said more gently remembering my tears. 'So they bring it back to their lodge and it sits at the head of the table that night... and afterwards they will wear its teeth.'

It was the pot that broke the spell: a terrible foundry-hiss of spitting soup that had the Indians on their feet, Marged shrieking, myself and Annie darting to the stove.

The meal was ready.

The brothers stood just beyond the door, staring in as through an invisible screen. Annie took down four white bowls, filled them and carried them out. From her pocket she took Marged's own silver spoon and fed the child. We men stood and drank, and smacked our lips and nodded as the cook's reward.

When Annie turned to us she opened her hands and then her arms in a gesture that meant 'no more' from Patagonia to the South Sea Islands and the Indians walked off into the trees without a gesture or a word.

'Well,' said Annie, 'something to tell Iorwerth, eh? When he gets back.'

But Iorwerth didn't get back. The short day wore out. At sundown there was a shot, so quickly followed by another it might've been its echo and we ran outside squinting at where the forest in the distance became lemon sky.

Nothing.

We were huddled round the stove when it happened, Marged dozing on her mother's knee as she sang to her, me trying to take in my lesson for the day. (My sister had taught at the school in our village once.)

'Read aloud,' Annie said.

I still know it by heart:

'Though here on earth men differ, in the grave
There's no distinction; all alike they have.
Then must the conqueror with the captive spread
On one bare earth as in the common bed...'

The last words were lost in the most horrendous clatter as some huge object struck the roof and slid down towards the eaves.

Marged screamed, Annie screamed but Annie had words to shout, 'Bobi! *Robert*! No!'

Too late. I'd played my sister's child long enough. My empty stomach was sick of it. I ran out, just in time to see the Indians in the last of the light. They turned before entering the cover of the trees. One held a rifle in either hand – because across his brother's shoulders was slung a fine young deer, lolling against the bear's teeth.

They looked over my head... made no gesture... were gone.

On our roof lay a huge buck. A pair of neat, pointed feet stretched out into thin air but the weight of the animal held it fast in its bed of white. There with a single hole through its heart.

'Why on the roof?' I asked, stupidly.

'Let's hope you can go to that college,' Annie said. 'You were never meant to live out here.'

It was nearly morning when Iorwerth dragged himself in, freezing, faint with defeat. Annie and I'd not slept, Marged was up again and we sat and ate slices off the roasting joint and drank tea and laughed and talked and ate again. The stove and the venison crackled. The lamplight shone in little Marged's green eyes and you could almost believe it was warm enough – at last warm enough – to melt whatever was frozen in behind them.

But it never was.

Fetish

The door eased a crack – she felt the cold breeze skim her exposed ankles – and the dog poked its head into the room just far enough to register her presence and make eye contact before dipping back out of sight.

In after-image she saw a slim white muzzle, the coarser, dark hair of drooping ears, a black nose.

She waited.

She found she was holding her breath.

On the screen before her, the new product range flickered; her finger had been forgotten on PgDn and when the scrolling halted, what steadied and coalesced was a thick leather collar embedded with inch-long brass-effect spikes. A flattened, heavy ring in matching yellow-metal protruded next to the buckle. From this a pop-up arrow appeared:

Matching Lead ! ! ! Only £12.99 ! ! ! See Item 105 B

The grey message and price flushed crimson and the arrow flashed in and out of existence. This was her son, Ross's work and very good it was too, she had to admit: each item cleverly cross-referenced to a set of related clothing, appliances, toys and printed matter, every possible thread of interest having been pulled taut as fishing line. No prospective customer had the opportunity for impulse buys denied him or her – most importantly the search through the merchandise was accomplished effortlessly, without volition. The collar and lead were neatly attached to leather belts, boots, gloves, basques, singlets and thongs and thence to masks, hoods and whips and clips. It was a corporate world away from that faint, photocopied sheet of tacky treats that had listed Patrick's back-bedroom stock – all those years ago. Maternal pride was obvious, had anyone been present to recognise it, in the way she nodded and grunted to herself, even as she closed down www.adamandeve.com.

Softly as her steel-tipped heels would allow, she made her way to the door; it was a doomed plan, this creeping up upon a creature whose reflexes were superior to her own but something childish and joke-loving inclined her to attempt it. She grabbed for the handle and yanked the door towards herself in what she hoped was one swift movement. The expanse of tarmac was empty save for a quartz baby Jaguar Sport. Beyond the hard-standing marked off as belonging to her own Unit 5, there was nothing much happening. Across the way, Piggott's the upholsterers were taking a delivery of gaunt beech skeletons that were to be fleshed out into chairs. As for the rest of them over there – Flintshire Foods, Alyn Electrical and Zeeta, the laboratory suppliers – any business they were conducting was undercover.

Over Evie's head, the single smear of clear sky healed shut in the heavy layers of cloud. A few hours ago, there'd been a hinting at snow in the darkness of her early start: now it seemed it was on its way. Of the dog there was no sign.

'What's up, Evie?'

Nigel Shuttleworth had approached unseen along the alley that divided her from Pacific Bathrooms. Taking the half-cigarette from his mouth, he positioned himself at the hole in the chain-link fence, stooping to line up his round and gleaming face full of freckles with her own. Despite the tan suit, cream shirt and brown silk tie, she guessed he'd been manhandling boxes of tiles or waste-traps in the warehouse only recently. Together with old nicotine, the breeze brought across the narrow space between them his sharp, fresh sweat – strong but not yet rank.

'Nothing – I just... nothing, Nigel. I thought I heard something.'

'You in on your own, then?'

He placed one hand carefully on the metal fence post now – she heard the click of the signet ring – and leaned in. Evie felt that if his head poked one centimetre further onto her property she'd be entitled to slap him. (Now where had that come from? She could *hear* the slap as her fingers whipped across his cheek, picture the sting as it registered in one already-watery eye.)

'You not got the girls in?' He craned his neck, attempting a search of the dim interior beyond the door.

'The girls' were a trio of pensioners: Pat, Dilys and Jean. It was Nigel's belief that a shoddily constructed and clumsily delivered innuendo from Nigel was a wondrous, post-menopausal thrill for Pat, Dilys and Jean. It was not.

'Oh they're in,' Evie assured him. 'Busy, we are. You?'

The sheen on his forehead and jowls dried as she watched. 'Oh, you know.'

A black SUV shot out of the alley and came to a stop within inches of Nigel's tan-jacketed behind. Choosing to ignore this, perhaps lacking the wit for a self-deprecating throwaway line, Nigel hurried around to the passenger side of the vehicle, concentrating on the difficult business of getting a car-door open, getting inside it. Dawn, the driver, dropped the window and grinned at Evie. 'Not to worry – I'll have him one of these days.'

Dawn's hair was the colour of their brass-effect clips, spikes, rings and clamps and it was shiny and unruffled by the wind. Only as the Shuttleworths disappeared in a long arc that took them across the front of their double unit and up towards Manor Lane did Evie notice the dog, staring out at her from the Chelsea Tractor's rear window.

Not having been rebuffed at its debut, the dog visited: most days for a week, every week for a month. Mid-mornings the undependable latch on the outside office door, after a couple of muffled blows, admitted the animal. Evie wondered at its use of the delicate muzzle as an instrument of force but then she knew little – no, she knew nothing about dogs. Her relationship with Ross's father had not been of the mock-Tudor semi, Labrador-keeping kind. Food: that must be the draw, she assumed. Around ten-thirty the sandwich van called, unit to unit. At adamandeve, 'the girls' and Evie, Les, and Ross, on those occasions he was honouring them with a show, bought lunch. Savoury, bready items were delivered to order – but for Pat, Dilys and Jean cakes were the thing. Half a dozen each to see them through the day's three breaks: anything oozing cream, chocolate, syrup and jam, these being preferred out of perversity, Evie felt, because they were just the wrong foodstuffs (there were no right foodstuffs) to have around the merchandise.

They discovered the dog did not do tricks.

'Go on,' Dilys told it, wafting a fragment of doughnut into the path of its intent gaze, 'give us a paw, then.'

The animal turned to a statue of itself.

'Oh, go on, 'ave it!' she laughed without rancour. The thrown dough-ball was snatched out of the air. At her elbow stacked, plastic bottles of Strawberry Luv Loob – their newest line – threatened collapse.

But when the cakes were all gone and Evie managed to chivvy the three back to making up the padded, discrete parcels – which, to be fair, they did with cackling dexterity and speed – the dog followed her to her cubby hole and lay down across her new Salvador Sapena wedges. The hair along its spine acted as a comforter to the open toes... gradually, the animal warmth of it registered in the trapped atmosphere of the desk-well... and there was a slight odour. It wasn't unpleasant, though far from sweet in the overpowering Strawberry Luv Loob style. A hint of nettles predominated over moist earthiness with a detergent aftertaste. The coat looked *washed*, the white body and legs catching the overhead light, turning them to silver, while the brown of its ears and back patches were copper sheened. Les, passing fully laden with a recent delivery, paused, watching her watching it.

'What sort is it?'

He shrugged, his always-wary, lined face unimpressed; he and his wife kept a German Shepherd, a picture of which, Evie

121

knew, resided in his wallet. 'Mongrel – no breed. Bit of collie, bit of spaniel... long legs, bit of lurcher, by the looks. Where's it come from?'

'Next door.'

'D'you want me chuck it back there?'

'It's doing no harm.'

'Well, once you let that lot feed it,' he gestured over his shoulder with his head, all that was free, 'you'll never get shut.'

'I know. Tell them, will you?'

'Me? You tell 'em.'

Across in the packing bay, Jean and Dilys were doubled up over their tables as Pat delivered some pronouncement on the new giant lipstick vibrator which, contrary to instruction, she had out of its box.

'Is it a he or a she?'

Les leaned over Evie's monitor. 'It's a he, poor sod.'

Dawn retrieved the dog late afternoon when the last éclair had been detached from the laminate cover of *Vegas Nights Reloaded* and 'the girls' were crowded into the tiny lavatory cubicle in preparation for homeward bus-journeys. Les was brushing up and Dawn made a great production of stepping around him, fanning imaginary particulate from the matt-apricot mask of her face. Evie guessed she and Dawn were about the same age but there the common ground fell sharply away. Dawn was hanging onto that desirable open verdict of *thirty-nineish?* (although not *quite* around her smoker's lips). But she was suspected of a holiday nip and tuck by Pat, who'd priced one up for Evie without being asked. Today Dawn was almost contained by tailored pedal-pushers and a wraparound clingy top in deep claret. *Five children, twin granddaughters*, said the ensemble, – *so?*

122

She gave Evie a single-frame smile and rattled her gold bangles at the reclining animal. 'Come on you! Sorry Evie. We've only had him since half-term. He's just settling down, doesn't know where he is.'

'Where did you get him?'

'Dog's home. Nice isn't he? You're all right, aren't you, Alvin?' Alvin remained couchant and yawned. 'Only young, he is. You can tell by the teeth.' She smiled again, lips tightly compressed this time. 'Alvin Starburst the kids call him.'

'Isn't it Alvin Stardust?'

'Well I should know.' Dawn paused for Evie to digest this puzzling put-down – but of course... *ownership*. 'They wanted a dog, they've been going on about it for ages, you know the way they do, and then who gets stuck with it? Oh yes, I'll have him out after school, Mum – that's our Claire – but now she's in the play, so here he is. He's having to come with us. You can guess what Nigel thinks....'

Nigel, unnoticed, had slipped in and was there beside Dawn, holding out the dog's leash. 'You forgot this. 'Lo Evie.' His eyes darted to Evie's screen with its disappointing column of figures and, sliding away, they lingered and narrowed over the anonymous Jiffys and packets. Only a reinforced carton (abandoned by a distracted Les on top of her filing cabinet) showed the added, felt-tip inscription: Sex Toy of the Month – Yellow Submarine Outies. No Batteries!!

Jacket flicked back, Nigel plunged both hands into his trouser pockets.

'Warm today – for the time of year,' Evie suggested. 'That snow came to nothing in the end. Les! *Les*! Get this moved, will you?'

123

For some reason, she took instantly against *Alvin* as a name for the visitor. It suggested comedy to Evie, and a bit part in the script at that. The dog was not an Alvin. This was a dignified creature, with a considering quality when it looked into a human face and a natural reticence in every movement. Walk through a doorway and it slipped in at your heels, waited to see where you'd settle before sliding gracefully from sitting to complete repose. It seemed not to sleep but fell instead into a watchful trance, staring at nothing – but move slightly or sigh deeply, and a pair of obsidian eyes were focused on you while its haunches tensed. Favoured by unregistered genes with drooping ears, these it could lower still further into a lawyer-like outline of curls, levelling the crown of the head for ease of stroking. This long, parti-coloured head she found a particular, velvet pleasure to the touch.

Though of no breed and with nothing to conform to, she thought Alvin a fine example of dog.

'What d'you think of Calvin?' she tried on Dilys. 'He's got used to bloody...' she lowered her voice to a whisper so as not to engage with the dog reclining at her feet, its eyes on her moving lips, 'Alvin now. It's not like a big change.'

'You can't go doing that.'

'I can. Watch me.'

'It'll get confused,' chipped in Pat, who should have been safely occupied mesmerising Jean with two dozen snaps of the interior of a studio apartment in Lloret del Mar. *This is the view out onto the patio that's a new block they're putting up you can just make it out there's that leather settee I told you they left us saw one just the same in fawn in Chester Sofa World six hundred pounds in the sales.* The images were being produced in a will-sapping stream from her overall pocket. 'Then one day 'er next door'll call 'im out the road and he won't come – and then get run over.' She had Jean's eyes widening in their crepe nests at the conjured drama.

'I might offer to buy him,' Evie said, surprising herself.

'What the 'ell for?'

'I like him.' She didn't need to look to reach down and massage the ridge of muscle that rested on Alvin/Calvin's shoulder-bones. The dog responded by pushing itself back into the pressure, forepaws braced.

Pat laughed. 'Like 'im?' It was always Pat's way to recruit others to her cause, even when she had no cause. The four of them sat along a crescent of pushed-together stools. She addressed Jean and Dilys, the reflections glinting combatively from the lenses of her bifocals: 'She *likes* 'im!' It wasn't by chance she and Evie always found themselves at opposite ends of the horn. 'Well, you don't want to let on to Wee Willie Winkie – does she?' Dilys shook her head, Jean excused herself with a good-natured shrug. 'That Nigel'll want top-dollar, won't 'e? 'e'll have got the mutt for nothing off the council and 'e'll want a pedigree price off you. You know they've laid off that nice girl from out the showroom? Things must be tight. Been with them since they started up, she has, and her and Dawn were best mates.' Pat, as far as Evie recalled, had never passed a single approving comment on that nice girl before.

'People have stopped buying houses, so they say, so they don't go doing up their bathrooms – not if they're not moving, see?' Dilys offered.

'Oh they're moving,' said Pat, 'but they're like us. They've got a bit of sense – moving abroad.'

'And when will that be?' Evie asked.

125

'I don't know, do I? 'e says we need to put a bit extra be'ind us. Work a bit more.'

Evie got to her feet. The dog did likewise. She brushed herself down and solemnly it watched each crumb's descent to the concrete before dabbing it up with a tongue-tip, performing a service. 'You took the words right out of my mouth,' she said. There was a half-completed order on the table, abandoned by one of them for afternoon tea. Inside she noted fifty Featherlite condoms, a tub of chocolate-flavour body-paint, a cinnamon-scented candle and a Sex Toy Of The Month vibrator, deep in its gold-cushioned, plastic box. The selection touched her with the merest hint of aversion – a hiccup of fishiness after having relished the paella – and she chose the candle to pick out and point at Pat for emphasis. 'Work a bit more.'

That night Evie ran over in her mind – testing, as it were – a homecoming with Calvin. She lived in a pink-washed bungalow she'd had built on an acre plot, sprawling level by level up the ascending ground – plenty of room in it for a dog, fields around – would he ride in the passenger seat of the Jaguar, upright, attentive to the passing miles? Once out of the Manor Lane Estate and turned away from the monstrous overhang of the aircraft factory, there were hedges and green bits – a farmy feel if not much in the way of farming going on – before the Jaguar was caught in the clutch-ageing judder that was a drive through Deeside's sprawl: Sandicroft delineated from Queensferry by a roundabout, Shotton from Connah's Quay by a railway. (But perhaps he'd prefer to doze the half-hour through, his muzzle on her thigh? She'd need to keep down the volume on Cerys Matthews and China Forbes.) At home up on the hillside, with its views to the river over all they'd just battled through, the dog would want to repossess the garden. He would check out the boundaries before accompanying her inside... she sees herself, wine-glass in hand, poking food out for him onto a dish... a brown pottery dish that says CALVIN... there goes the ping of the microwave, the scent of potato and melting cheese but she ignores them, choosing to watch the bowl of his food skitter like a puck over the terracotta tiles, worked by Calvin's random nudges and prods... Later she is in the cane lounger, watching from the shelter of the conservatory, as the sun goes down and turns the Dee to polished steel. There is the lighthouse to look for. Sometimes, just before it dies, the sun will glance off the West Kirby lighthouse on the far, green peninsula – and even if it doesn't, even if the sky turns to heather and puce and the thunder rolls up the wide estuary, then there are the cheerful, always-reborn bubbles to follow as they spend themselves at the surface of her Hardy's chardonnay. Though a daydream, it keeps faith with the season so that the hydrangeas in the borders are heavy headed and brown, the evening short and rapidly failing – but without even a hint of chagrin. Inside, where they will soon be driven, she and Calvin, there are bright lamps and Joan Armatrading on old vinyl: '*You called me all the way from America...*'

'Mum?'

'Hello, Ross. Didn't expect to see you.'

'I've been calling! Shit, where've you been? They said you left at three.' His lean, handsome face with its beautiful cheekbones is expressive of *something* for once.

'Just out for a walk. All the way to the Abbey and back. I didn't mean to go so...'

'Why can't you take your phone?'

'Forgot it, didn't I?'

'Are you all right – are you stoned, or what? It's nearly dark!' He, like she, is a child of the cramped lower ground, the streets, roads and huddled terraces – has never been reconciled to this elevation of realty, this domestic isolation.

'It's fine. I had the dog.' *Yes she would have the dog.*

As if on cue, Calvin is upright, showing Ross his teeth.

All morning the deep throb of the juggernaut's diesel had tested the panels of her office wall. To ease a head throbbing in sympathy, rather than out of curiosity, Evie printed off the orders that had come in over night and walked across to deposit them in Jean's tray – of the three, only Dilys looked up, smiled – and rather than return to her desk, she wandered outside. A stiff gust was coming from the direction of Pacific Bathrooms and on it acrid engine fumes... but beyond and above them, the empty sky over Hawarden Hill was blue as chicory flowers. Clean-looking. Unlike the yard where drinks cans, crushed by the Jaguar's and others' wheels, had welded themselves to the tarmac and paper and plastic waste clawed at the chain-link. There'd been spindly saplings and shrubs planted along a grass perimeter... years ago, when she'd first leased the unit. Where had they gone? *When* had they gone? In the far corner, where Les had his steel bins and backless smoking chair, was that a stake lying in the hardened mud? Something that had once supported a young tree?

Nigel, bolstered still further by a padded jacket, although over the same old straining tan suit, came striding to her. 'Sorry 'bout this. Just getting rid of surplus stock. Thought we'd have a clear out and then... y'know, come the spring, new designs. Y'know.'

Evie glanced in as a couple of kids not Ross's age manhandled the last asymmetrical, corrugated-cardboard coffin up the ramp. GRANADA SPA BATH – SHANKLEY BROS – STOKE ON TRENT. *Surplus stock* looked very similar to entire stock. Dawn was hanging around, chatting to the removers, pretending not to notice her husband or Evie. From inside the warehouse, an unseen agent brought the roller-door down with a metallic clash. Then with some yelling the ramp was heaved up and slammed and bolted into position. Dawn flinched with each sound, still did not turn.

'Sorry,' Nigel said again, gesturing at the dog at Evie's heels. 'He must've got out – with the lads being back and forth. We *are* trying to...'

'Do you want me to buy him off you?'

A thick belch of exhaust threatened them as the truck inched out of the yard. For an instant Nigel's face was obscured – but only for an instant.

'I've said I'm sorry.' Now it was peevish. Here was a glimpse of unglazed Nigel, Evie had seen many times in a long acquaintance. 'I stopped coming to get him 'cos Dawn said it wasn't a problem. You only had to say.' Down on his knees he probed beneath the unravelling fence with one powerful arm in an attempt to grab the dog's collar and hoick it to him.

'Don't! No!' Calvin made no sign of co-operation, no desire to become Alvin. He backed away.

'Ah, fuck it!' Nigel said, straightening up, panting. 'I'll have to come round.'

'No. Really. I'm serious – what do you want for him? Really.'

'Yeah?' There was mud on his knees but he ignored it;

129

some well-used sixth-sense had him glancing over one shoulder. 'Uh-h... well.'

Finally Dawn turned, was heading toward them, was almost on them...

'I'll give you five hundred,' Evie said.

...was there.

'*What*?'

'What?' Dawn asked.

'What's the next colour for bathrooms?' Evie said.

Dawn frowned. 'White, same as always. Come here Alvin – get yourself through this fence.' The dog waited for some other word from some other speaker – one that was not forthcoming – before it dropped onto its belly, wriggling forward, the fence-wire combing furrows along its back. When dog and Dawn were safely started toward the side door, Evie held up her hand to the lingering Nigel, fingers spread.

Five, she mimed. But even as she walked back in to find Ross, to pick a fight with Pat, to demand Les get out here and clear up all this sodding plastic and paper from out of this cesspit of a yard (*Christ, what's got into her? Nothing, Pat says, that's her problem*), she knew it was a losing bid.

'Won't have it. Sorry. Doesn't matter a stuff to me but Dawn says no.' Nigel watched the three pink-overalled backs of 'the girls' as they bent to their processing and sorting of festive luxuries: variety packs of edible thongs, fun-fur lined handcuffs. 'You were winding me up, weren't you?'

'No. I wasn't.'

'My mistake.'

The dog had not made its looked-for appearance. Dawn's prohibition, she guessed. Nigel seemed in no hurry to leave. In the absence of a chair he was forced to lean against the wall, long arms folded, puffy cheeks subsiding, a mournful orang-utan. The silk tie was pastel stripes today but marked with some darker spillage and knotted on the uncomfortable side of tight. No wonder his breathing seemed too rapid for a man at rest. Pity for him came out of nowhere but it was unwelcome and Evie batted it away together with a flash of intuition: that she was simply picking up a trace of what Nigel felt for himself. (Patrick could do that, she remembered, slink from bluster to self-abasement in an instant, demanding she shadow the movement with appropriate indulgences, expressed loyalty). Nigel sniffed loudly as a prelude to: 'to be honest I'd have taken it. Best offer I've had all week – only offer I've had all week. I tell you, this bathroom game's not what it used to be. They've all got the new suites that want them. And nobody's going to spend on a Jacuzzi when it's coming up to Christmas.' His spongy underlip protruded, enveloping the rawly shaved upper. 'How are Santa's naughty little helpers?' he called out, but none of them acknowledged the question. Somewhere off to one side, Les's tinny radio was jangling nerves with premature Christmas tunes. 'It's all right for some. Let's face it, what you're flogging here – ha! ha! – well, it never goes out of fashion, does it?'

'A thousand,' Evie said.

He gave a decent impression of not having heard now. 'They say the aircraft place might be on short time, next.'

'A thousand,' said Evie. 'In cash.'

'You must be mental. You can get a pedigree for a lot less than that.'

'It's my money.'

Carefully, he backed around a pallet stacked with mesh cages, small padded envelopes of delicate items awaiting final transport to the bay where the Parcel Force van would dock. He made for the door, keys and change rattling in his pockets, shaking his head.

Silly bitch said the headshake.

Or *no*.

'Don't tell me that again!' Ross is loud with disbelief. 'This is – what? Oh, this has got to be... I mean. You're mad, right?'

'I'm out of it, Ross. Trust me. It's going to happen. Now can we talk...'

'No! I don't want to hear.'

Evie's lounge is mainly white: the Hong Kong rug's hand-cut wool pile is as near white as dammit, the chairs and sofas are covered in white heavy cotton, the curtains on the four sets of patio doors are of raw silk, as are the cushion covers and throws. The walls, apart from the unplastered brick chimney breast, are washed in Old Porcelain White, while the pair of console tables and shelves on either side of the fireplace are constructed of solid, limed oak. To see Ross pacing up and down this room with a full, open can of Stella Artois is not relaxing.

'The business is yours. It was always going to be. What did you think it was all for? It was always for you, love...'

'But not *now*. To be honest, Mum, I don't want it now. Jesus, you're not sick are you?' His expression is changed: the Patrick part, the features that spring out at the slightest opposition along the jaw-line and around the widening nostrils, dissolve back into his own familiar face. Here again is the twenty-four year Ross – here also is the thirteen-year-old Ross, caught scraping away at his top lip for signs of stubble... the ten-year-old Ross with a bleeding mouth from a schoolyard fight. Evie has to, cannot help but, warm to the effect – even as another part of her recognises it as no more than a camera trick of capture and fixation, one performed in the chambers of her heart.

'No, I'm not sick. Just sick of this, if you like.'

On the cushion beside her is a small, expensive bag. Evie pops the clasp and removes a masculine leather bill-fold; from it she removes a piece of printed, folded paper. 'Here,' she offers it to him, 'this is what I have in various accounts.'

He takes it from her after a show of reluctance, looks at her, checks back with the figures and whistles. 'Way to go, Mum. Do I get this as well?'

'No you bloody don't! What I'm telling you is, that'll last me. I'm knocking on, you know. And if it doesn't – well, I'll just sell this place, get something smaller. Downsize – it's the new black.'

'But *why*?'

'I've told you why. Fed up with everything. Had enough. Gonna stop. Game over.'

'Is it...' Evie can see and feel his attempt at comprehension. 'Is it something to do with this crap with the Shuttleworths? Les says *she* was out there this morning, giving one of our deliveries a right bollocking, just for blocking something or other. Because if it is, all you have to do is wait it out. I mean I don't pretend to understand... about the dog. I don't want to get into it – you know what I think. But the Shuttleworths, they've had it. The estates office is advertising their lease next month. They're gone, any minute.'

'I know.'

'What then? Christmas? Once we get that over...'

133

'Look, I've said.' She laughs in an attempt to candy an unpalatable half-truth. 'D'you reckon when I was your age I thought oh, right, I'll just spend the next eighteen years of my life making up packets of stuff in plain wrappers? Grimy goodies for a load of sad wankers and wannabe tarts?'

'*Mum!*'

'No I didn't. And yeah, that is my opinion of the business. It was then and it is now.' It *certainly* is now, she sees, but she has no intention of letting the talk go any further in that direction. 'The Internet made it bigger not different. We're not selling baby-clothes, love.' But he is her son and she his mother and that is *definitely* as far as they go. The open can of Stella is useful, though hazardous – he can down it, not have to meet her eyes. 'Don't worry, I haven't got religion. Just bored.' Almost to herself, although it isn't a novel or previously unvoiced thought, she says. 'I don't know, perhaps I only made a go of it to spite Patrick.'

Soon after, he leaves – for a flat she has bought him and a girl called Martijna Evie she has helped get a visa for. She waves him off with good humour, on her side at least, and returning, kneels on the rug, her bare knees sinking into the deep rough wool. What is beneath her palm is much softer: the silken, hot flank of the dog as it stretches in the heat from the fire. With closed-eyed concentration she takes her hand to the topmost vertebrae in the dog's neck, begins the downward slide again... and again.

'You hungry, Calvin?'

He follows her into the kitchen where she takes a slab of purplish steak from the fridge. Despite the chill, its sweet-fatty odour seems very strong, especially as she rarely buys red meat for herself. It causes the dog to lick his lips, giving a flash of perfect, and very long, white canines – well up to the mastication of raw sirloin. But at the last moment she changes her mind and freezes mid-action just on the point of placing the meat onto Calvin's steel plate. She hooks out the kitchen stool with one foot, sits down and begins, with a sharp knife, to carve the lump of flesh.

This she drops into his waiting jaws, for the sheer pleasure of feeding him, piece by succulent piece.

The Garden of Early Delights

He wasn't my first – I was going to say patient, but of course I don't have patients anymore. I have clients. When I began counselling he'd be only my third or fourth counsellee, something like that. One of the few to set foot in my new house – and the only one to be admitted to the garden. (*Where I am sitting, my glass clutched to my face, and through it I see him as distinctly as I see that ragged groundsel rooted in nothing between the cracks, though it is another season entirely now.*)

He would've come via Steph, a local G.P. and a friend. There was a muddle, I recall, involving Steph's practice manager and holidays: some lack of a forwarded note – and the patient, the client, well, he seemed to be under the misapprehension I was still a registered consultant psychiatrist.

And we were both wrong.

'Dr Merrick?'

'Yes. No. It's Mrs Merrick. Although not for long... and you are?'

'I think you should be expecting? Yes?'

I have to suppress a smirk – then a lorry the size of a holiday home thunders past forcing a pause. He blinks, once only, at the height of the assault on our ears and is quicker than I at cutting in as the racket diminishes. 'I have appointment with you today. Two-thirty – Nicky Kwok?'

'Of course.' I back up the narrow passage. 'Come in, please – mind the step.' The sudden step *down* from the street comes as a shock if you don't mention it; the new visitor rattles his or her teeth, is mocked by the lack of footing, gets pissed off. 'This is where I... go in, please... take either chair.'

It's small, the space I direct him to: a thin low room with a central empty fireplace and a pair of blue armchairs, separated by one of those Perspex coffee tables that looks as if it isn't quite there. But it is there and for a very good reason. That not-quite-there obstacle gives just those few extra seconds I'll need to get out of the room. Look at my published papers: you'll see.

'OK Mr Kwok...'

It's his turn to master a smile. 'It's Dr. But Nicky best – unless there is some rule?'

'Nicky, then.'

The thing is, I'd assumed female Nicky – not this tall (very tall for a Chinese) young man who bows his head in assent and then bows again to get under the oak beam and so to his chair. I close the door and quell the low Spring sun with the blind. When I turn, he is already in his seat as directed....

I note jeans, clean but very worn, and good leather boots only half-laced. He has a big face. Not a big head, which is a perfectly normal size and covered in very short black hair. No, rather there's some small proportional problem with the dispersion of his features: the eyes too widely set, the distance between upper lip and nose virtually the same as that between lower lip and chin. The overall impression is too open, too childlike and he is twenty-six – now where did that snippet come from? – and will never mature to handsomeness now.

'Ordinarily I'd have your notes by this time,' I say. 'But the surgery hasn't managed to... it'll be the Easter holiday. I've spoken to your GP of course.' A lie, but *clients* don't like to think of themselves as an e-mail, a ten-word electronic referral. 'She said... well, she seemed keen that you come and see me. We talked about you, obviously, and I'll have it all by the next time you come.' Only at this does he look up as though actually listening. '*If* you come again. If you think it'll help.'

Now he appears to be studying the titles on the bookshelves that fill one wall. My own trio are carefully prominent within his eye-line, both from ego and a professional desire to reassure. The sanctification of print has, in the past, helped along more than a few miraculous remissions – I'd never claim cures – in this fertile, degree-growing river valley of Oxfordshire. 'You're a scientist of some sort, is it?'

'A theoretical physicist.' He is hanging onto his words, chewing them in his cheeks though whether from relish or fear only the forthcoming session will tell. 'A physicist and a...' here embarrassment throws up yet one further barrier, 'a harpist.'

'You're a musician! The two often go together.'

'An *artist*,' he corrects, 'calligrapher, you'd say it.'

'I see. But at the moment you can do neither?'

'Yes,' he agrees and draws up his long legs and draws in his arms from the wooden armrests and hunches, if one with such a rangy physique can be said to hunch. 'No good. At anything. Not any more.'

'But this isn't why you consulted Dr O'Neil is it? Wasn't there something more, well, more immediate?'

'Yes.'

Beyond the double glazing another giant truck throws deeper gloom over us – my house faces north-east and opens directly onto the pavement – and so for the first instant I fail to take it in... then I see that, in leaning forward, Nicky Kwok has opened his palms in the ancient, universal gesture of appeasement. And that both of them, from the mound of his lemon-skinned thumb to the base of his long slim fingers, are red raw.

'May I see?' He extends the right hand but turns his head and torso away, reminding me of my hospital days and the patients preparing themselves for injection... giving up the part you intend to assault whilst the rest of the body prepares to leave the room. 'I won't hurt you. I just needed to see the extent of... I won't touch, I promise.'

To the bookshelves he says, 'It's no problem. But I have also... stomach illness. Complaint. It can make breath sour.' Courteously he exhales at two copies (one English, one American Edition) of *Self-harm and the Young Offender* by Jill Merrick.

I place my own hand beneath his and, gently as I can, slant it towards the window. The redness is now revealed not as a uniform patch of flayed flesh but a series of abrasions with some evidence of puckered healing and scabbing over. Generalised inflammation is present. There is also a livid river of congealed blood along the life-line. 'That looks painful.'

'The other is same.'

I sit back so he might relax again and turn to face me. 'I believe Dr O'Neil began by treating you for a skin condition. Some sort of allergy was suspected? Nickel, I think was mentioned – an allergy to nickel. It would've been my first try. Nickel allergy is quite common.'

'Yes.'

'But... but now she's having second thoughts... the steroids having had no effect? I see there's some evidence of mild secondary infection. So-o... you'll have a wait to get to see a dermatologist, I guess?'

'Is there any point?' he asks sharply. 'If you've talked to Dr O'Neil you know she thinks this waste of time because... because...'

'Because you're doing it yourself. *Are* you doing it yourself?'

He does smile now: teeth on show for the first time, square and strong though irregular, a perfect correlation with the rangy physique. They speak of a well-nourished childhood – and now something else surfacing for the first time, a sense of humour. 'I think if some other person doing it, they should be here and not me,' he says.

'Quite.' I wait. He is un-bothered by silence. 'So are you aware of its happening? The damage.'

'No.'

'Mm.'

Two figures – shadows just beyond the drawn blind – catch his attention. Their muffled laughter dwindles away in the direction of Abingdon town centre and is absorbed into background hum.... When first coming here I had doubts as to

141

this room's suitability for consulting, facing onto the main road as it did, every passer-by only inches distant from the expected bubble of privacy. But now I appreciate its therapeutic plus point: it connects with the outside world. Families pass, loving or quarrelling, couples, canoodling or sulking. Singletons. And all against a backdrop of the noisy, working life of a humanely-scaled and well-preserved pocket borough. Abingdon, with its expensive riverbank, streets-full of medieval buildings in a better state of repair than when first erected, has to be *the* place for Oxonians who find Oxford just too cool.

I'm one of its refugees.

As is Nicky Kwok, who now sits immobile.

'Why don't we leave the question for the moment – of your hands, I mean? Why don't we talk about what was happening before all this started. How long ago would that be?'

'Do you want to know when I went to Dr O'Neil?'

'Not necessarily. Most people experience symptoms – put up with things or don't notice that something's wrong... Only later do they say to themselves, *Oh, that's when it happened* – or maybe they say *Yes! That's when things changed.*'

His expression is dubious but he thinks it over, examining his hands again in the reasonable hope of a visual clue. Something that I can't see in the left palm needs to be explored, held up. I don't look at it. I try to give him ease in his quest by busying myself: smoothing down the black fabric of my skirt, removing a bright thread that, I realise, has moulted from his multi-coloured sweater. 'I think,' he says to the hand rather than to me, 'it would be six months – yes, at least six months. March now? Well April nearly – yes?' His speech becomes more difficult to differentiate just when I'm confident I'm getting the knack of it. 'In October... back.' (It could be 'last' though.) 'I went to see my... grandfather, my mother's father. In Melbourne. After that.'

'It appeared immediately after that?'

'Yes. First week home.'

'Well, you must've asked yourself if there was a connection. You're a scientist. You must've wondered if you'd been in contact with – what? a pathogen, perhaps... or some sort of sensitisation process? Surely you thought that?'

His nod is barely perceptible. Found out. In my experience, the more intelligent the subject the more likely it is to have them disclaiming their own knowledge, their own fears. Later, these same are part of another subgroup: the overly triumphant at defeating help.

'But I'll bet you've done a pretty thorough search – a lot of reading up, eh? The Net? You type in skin+lesions, negotiate your way around fifty thousand hits...'

'More.'

'A hundred thousand hits, then – and you've drawn a blank?' I pause for a spate of further admissions – that don't come. 'Religious, are you?'

'Not Christian.'

'But – *of course* – you know about stigmata? These are holes in the hands – they bleed constantly and don't heal. They're the nail marks of Christ's crucifixion. That's a possible explanation – though whether it's a blessing or a punishment–' He doesn't pursue the unprofitable theme of belief. 'You can also get them in the feet. There are cases where the sword wound – supposedly the one made in Christ's side – erupts as well. But you've read up on all this by now, haven't you?' He doesn't claim he hasn't. *There's hopeful.* 'You just can't see a connection with your own problem?' Nothing. *Don't let him slither away now.* 'Tell me about Melbourne, then. How did that go?'

'It was... happy visit.'

'Really?'

'Of course.'

'All good then?'

'Yes.'

Oh dear.

While Nicky Kwok describes the goodness in some detail – the prosperous Cantonese *emigré* father, project managing a huge Government building-push in Melbourne... the mother's business importing silks, begun as a hobby and now become so successful she threatened to overtake her husband in dollar-earning capability... the aged and ailing grandfather who despite his son-in-law's desire to accommodate him in the family mansion, lives in the pool house. In my head (though I listen attentively) there run those other lines with their stale aftertaste of disinformation: *Oh Galuppi, Baldassaro, this is very sad to find! I can hardly misconceive you; it would prove me deaf and blind; But although I take your meaning, 'tis with such a heavy mind!*

Even when it's delivered with all the concentrated sincerity of a Nicky Kwok.

'You understand I'm just a counsellor?' I demand. 'Not a physician. I'd be willing to try to help – if we can agree on the value of discourse. Do we?'

'How can I tell? If this goes...' *Excellent. Rude boy, Nicky. Talk to the red palms, is what you're wanting to say to me.*

'Right answer.'

Long after Nicky Kwok's first hour was run away and he'd donned the soft cotton disposable gloves that, he explained, he was now forced to wear to drive, the phrase 'family mansion' returned to me. I was edging up the stairs (which open in a cupboard in the left corner of my consulting room), my arms laden with assorted items that find their way down and need to be put back into position... that's something you learn quickly when coming to inhabit much-reduced premises. Never go through any door without checking there's not a book, a coffee mug, an article of clothing, an unanswered official letter that should be coming with you. I've been here over a year now, a straight move (via 'the clinic') from four floors of prodigal proportions in north Oxford to a minute, terraced cottage comprising kitchen, bathroom, bed-sitting room and consulting room. Even this makes No 80, The Vineyard sound more spacious, more normally domestic, than it is.

There's one of those cobbled-together local histories on my bookshelves, all sepia photographs and hand-drawn maps. 'Notwithstanding the almshouses in Long Alley and a morsel of Abbey that Henry VIII overlooked', mine is 'the oldest inhabited dwelling in Abingdon'. My house. *The thin pink house*, as I tell patients – or the friends who decided to stick with me instead of going with Rory. *The thin pink house with the purple door straight onto the pavement*. It's the oldest in the town. That step down from street level's a bit of a give-away, apparently. How long do you have to be there, how long for the rest of town to raise itself around you by the gradual accretion of a full eleven inches? And it's still happening. Beneath the road with its thunderous traffic stream lies another, the River Stert, and into the marshy bosom of this lost Thames tributary, I am gradually being clasped. Not subsidence so much as settlement. 'Not useful,' it said in the surveyor's report, 'to talk of a building of this degree of antiquity as subsiding. But movement has certainly taken place and in all likelihood continues.' Subsidence, settlement, indefinable movement? Suction, more like, a slow uneven pull down into the very mud of which most of the house is made. And don't be misled by that terrace concept. 80 The Vineyard had been here a *long* time – the buildings each side of me are Regency and welcome only because they're holding me up.

'If you think,' said Rory, my ex, 'I'm taking on responsibility for this little money-pit, you're wrong. You can get a fifty-year lease on a flat in Summertown for what they're asking for it. Show some sense, Jill.'

When Nicky Kwok left after that first session my impulse was to reacquaint myself with a passage from Ian Wilson's excellent *Stigmata*. But this was carefully packed up and sealed with duck-tape, twelve miles away in an Oxford attic along with many other indispensable repositories of psychiatric lore. So I walked out into my garden, picking up my notebook and a glass of water on the way (*it is recommended that on those occasions when an alcoholic drink might be usual a different sort of beverage be substituted, the lack of alcoholic 'hit' to a seasoned and prolonged drinker being virtually imperceptible*). Back to the sun, I perched on the low retaining wall that separated grass from newly flagged yard and read.

NK, the patient (sic), is a twenty-six-year-old Chinese man presenting with scarification of both hands. He displays every sign of acute anxiety – the lacerated condition of his hands, he claims, being a cause of this anxiety rather than its symptom. There are indicators of social isolation. Attention seeking cannot be ruled out at this stage, nor the possibility of dual diagnosis (drug abuse plus?). Although highly intelligent he appears unwilling to admit the obvious and most simple explanation for his predicament, namely that it is...

The pencil dropped from my fingers even as I was in the process of adding to this sorry stuff *self-mutilation*.

'Nicky Kwok.' I said the name out loud to get it to settle, to insist in some more substantive way that here was another person: an actual other person, apart from Jill Merrick. I'd been having a bit of trouble with this one.

It's a small and shrinking island I washed up on. I wasn't always alone here but the two others in my party struck out for the mainland a while back – leaving me to hang around with my unread Bible, complete works of Shakespeare and Browning's poems, my extra book. And until a year, five months and three days ago, there was also that single, sanctioned luxury – an unlimited supply of booze.

Rory I know pretends to me and to everyone else and to Rory that it was the drink that did it. (*Oh Galuppi, Baldassaro, this is very sad to find!*) It wasn't. We *both* drank, the way so many people in their forties do, drank more and then drank more, more often. We drifted into drink in exactly the same way I've seen friends drift into obsession with global warming, the ocular health of the Third World or restoring that modest *manoir* inland from La Rochelle. Bit by bit, year by year. Natural predilection is rewarded with social acceptance, often with psychological easement. Sometimes both. So what did we have to choose from, Rory and me? It wasn't an extensive list. We were as far as we were going in our respective spheres, and Jack was in his second year at Edinburgh and had hardly needed either a mother nor a father since (at the age of ten and a half) he'd presented himself at Balliol's SCR to discuss the fairness

147

or otherwise of Oxford Entrance. Please excuse a mother's desire to tell you Jack was, at seventeen, offered a place by Balliol *and* Trinity, Cambridge and chose Edinburgh himself.

Drink became our shared pastime, never interfering with workaday life. Rory's lectures continued to be delivered in his dry, rapid-concept-fire for which he is so famous. I never presented myself at the hospital as anything but sober. Getting wrecked is like any other form of physical activity; perform it frequently and the body adapts. A litre of Beaune and enough water before bedtime and the next day you're not caught slurring your words.

A pastime I called it. Then Rory found a new and absorbing pastime – Farah.

Didn't drink!

And a litre and then several litres of Beaune was all I had left.

You know the only trouble with wine? Good, bad or just plain outrageously filthy wine? Red, white, slatey, flinty, fruity or *frizzante* wine? It's a fuck-awfully slow way to get drunk. Rory went home with Farah and I snuggled up with Smirnoff and nobody – absolutely nobody – was to blame...

Memory becomes problematic at this point. There are days when I honestly have no idea whether I was struck off during my stay in the clinic or just before it. Today is one of those days.

Nicky left and I sat out there in my long strip of a garden and pretty soon abandoned any of pretence at note-writing. I dropped pen and paper and wandered over to pick up the trowel embedded in the new border, and it came free with the scent of black alluvial earth. It was as clear and hopeful a spring day as will ever be granted – as Nicky Kwok had correctly asserted, nearly April. *Correct, Nicky and about the only thing you said I could believe*. In the far corner beneath the kitchen window, the leaves of the double-red peony were starting to show – and strips of pansies were over-running their plastic containers and in desperate need of bedding out along the line of the path. That climbing rose was also causing concern. The first arrival after my clearance of the plot, now it drew me to it. On the far trellis (there were two other green-painted panels of trelliswork nearer the back door) I stopped to examine the sprouts of growth...

Rosa foetida bicolor – Austrian Copper. Something was not quite right. For a start it was looking just too full of itself – too healthy by far. Not a hint of laxity in its branches (in fact it gave every impression of independence from the system of ties that were meant to be its support) nor of any incubating disease of its new foliage. Of course I had my misgivings even before I'd got it home. It had been the product of a chance visit to the little nursery in Radley; a hand-painted sign had drawn my car down a track to the half-acre enterprise behind a post-war bungalow. I think it was without decision on my part – but the significant portion of action is so.

The name of the place alone should warn me off: Evergreens – Hardy Plants, Shrubs and Perennials. Run by a couple of knowledgeable old birds, it isn't going to cater for my sub-species of horticulture.

'A red rambler,' I describe it to the shorter, fatter, pleasanter of the two. 'Not a big flower, but lots of them and lots of scent too. Very *heavy* fragrance. Old variety.'

'A name?'

'Obviously not.'

'When you say old – I mean 'old-fashioned' is a technical term used by people like Hillier, say.'

I've no idea who Hillier is nor any intention of asking. 'It was in cultivation at least forty years ago,' I say.

They exchange a warm and wicked glance. I have them down as sisters, both khaki-trousered, National Trust sweat-shirted – but by that look, I know. It has *lover* written all over it.

Can a single poly-tunnel and all those carefully hand-labelled pots add up to a business? Of course it can't. 'Evergreens' is an adored, much spoilt only daughter.

'Try her with *Austrian Copper*, Barb,' says the taller Ms Evergreen. 'She won't go wrong with *Austrian Copper*. If it's not the one she's looking for, she still won't be bringing it back.'

I wouldn't be taking *Austrian Copper* back. Not-Barb was right. But the moment I came across the real thing (more crimson than scarlet in flower, languishing in habit, silvered by mildew at the end of every season) it was coming out.

Nicky Kwok missed his next session. He had both my numbers, didn't ring: I mentioned it to Steph while we were lunching at The Upper Reaches, watching the mallard drakes on the Thames down below... 'Well, perhaps you *healed* him with one shot,' she said, the callousness of this remark her revenge for my bad taste in mentioning work. 'Bit sad, though, isn't it? He's – *my God*! Have you got to the risotto layer of this yet? It's orgasmic!' She continued with a full mouth. 'He's absolutely brilliant, apparently, our Dr Kwok. First degree at fifteen. The college made him a Fellow three years ago. They'd pay for his treatment like a shot. But he's got a bad case of principles, to go with everything else. So no comfy little clinic. Pity – he was tipped for – *Chir-ist-t*! The aubergine – what have they done to this? Eat some of yours. Eat it now.'

I told her about Evergreens, to make up. But Barb's meticulously-bleached little moustache I left out. And that look passed from Barb to Not-Barb that had pricked me like a thorn.

A week later there was Nicky again at my door. Same jeans, same jumper. Very clean. (He must wash them each night). White cotton gloves. Ditto.

He was staring at the new sign I'd had put up only that day: J Roberts, Counselling.

'Mrs Merrick?'

'Well I was. I've reverted to my maiden name of Roberts. I've divorced.' I had meant to say *I'm* but I liked that *I've*. It was positive, active.

He passed into my consulting room, juggling with *R*oberts, R*oberts* and mumbling something about 'sorry last' and 'note'. Other polite lies.

I found him in the chair he had taken previously, his eyes already closed and head thrown back: anxious to begin. His face was turned away and I was noting the smoothness of an Oriental profile in contrast to the definite ins and outs of a European, when I was caught off-guard. With that difficult intonation, he begin to recite, 'Richard Brooke Roberts – it was this man discovered in 1939 that the fissioning uranium atom does not release all its neutrons at same time – and understanding of these delayed neutrons played important part in control mechanism of nuclear reactors. He was Roberts.'

'Ah, poor old Uncle Dickie – we always knew he'd come to a bad end.' This got his eyes open at least. 'Joke. It's a very common name where I come from. Is this your area? Nuclear fission?'

'Nuclear fission,' he said seriously, 'has very bad reputation.

151

I would never.... My work is concerning the weak force. You know?'

'No.'

'It is the important force. It is...' I watched his courteous casting around for words at the base level of understanding. 'It is the force that stops some... things becoming other... things. It allows for them to keep their... selves.'

Just how precisely, I wondered, was I being teased? I had to resist the temptation to lean across, to tap him on the arm and acknowledge the hit. 'Sounds like my sort of force,' I said. 'Would you like to begin with your work, now you've mentioned it? The pressure of it, perhaps?' His stare was straight through me to the rectangle of brightness. 'So – another beautiful day again – why don't we do this in the garden? It's quite private.'

He followed me out, but uneasily.

That fresh quality in the spring sunshine had transformed my strip of urban Thames Valley into something vivid and aggressively vital. A sky of clear blue curved over the green, both cheerful and crude as unmixed poster paint. 'Let me give you the grand tour.'

My second joke. What we were looking at was a simple space, sixty feet long and fifteen wide; a rectangle of paving narrowed to a central path between two lawns in need of their first cut and strips of flower border. As yet the only flower colour came from the bought-in pansies' yellow, mauve and purple-black.

They should have been grown from seed and next year would be.

A high wall, just above head height, part gold-grey local stone, part brick surrounded the whole thing – although along the right hand side this was stretched to two storeys and became the windowless rear wall of a long barn. I gestured Nicky Kwok to a seat lined up against it. His anxiety was palpable in his darting pupils and high, clenched shoulders. 'This behind us – it's just a barn – I think it was once something to do with my cottage, when this land was orchard or vineyards belonging to the Abbey. Now it goes with next door and it's full of furniture the Lindops are storing for a friend. Nice couple, the Lindops – perfect neighbours, in fact. They both work in Oxford and the house is empty between seven in the morning and seven at night. On the other side, there's a Mr Pereira. We, that's me and the Lindops, are a bit worried about him. I've only seen him twice and not for months. Arms dealer, we reckon. At the far end– where you can see the trellis on the wall? – well beyond there's a plot of overgrown ground. Wild. One of those bits that's got hemmed in and doesn't seem to be anybody's. *So there's nobody to overhear us while we're sitting here.*'

He sighed just the once. Closer to and in better light I saw how deep were crescents of plum beneath his eyes.

'Is there any improvement – in your hands?'

Today he had not taken off the gloves.

'No. I have thought... about what we said. My time with Grandfather and... but no, no better.'

'You mentioned your grandfather – he lives in the pool house in the garden, your parents' garden?'

'Yes.'

'Why?'

For the first time that day, he smiled. 'My mother ask why, all the time.'

'And he says?'

'He says nothing.'

'I see. And what do you have to say?'

'I say nothing. With him.' Every muscle tensed for standing – yet he remained.

Despite my assurance of privacy our speech had been low and now declined to stillness. A song thrush settled on the grass at the base of the far wall. She – I always assume she for a thrush, *he* for a robin – she picked along the angle so formed, feeding I thought until I saw the collection of dried stems, the prize she flew away with. 'This is my parents' garden,' I told Nicky Kwok. 'Or will be. I've tried to recreate it. It was their garden in Wales – where I grew up. They're dead now.'

Correctly, he inclined his head. 'Why do you make it?'

'For myself. I just needed to – at the time. Last year. For them, perhaps, as well. They lived – the four of us lived, I had a sister – we lived half way up the valley. Another valley, I've just realised! But not like here. It was... how can I explain? Not as smart. A bit less cared-for than here, if you get me, but very beautiful. Trees and heather. Fields with more gorse than grass in them. There was a quarry up behind us and the trucks from it turned everything white with dust in summer. That was my father's work – he kept the trucks on the road, which was much better than trying to farm... which is what he'd done before that.'

'He worked hard I think.' It wasn't a question – in fact, he was staring down between his own knees, those hands hanging slackly in their white cotton.

'Yes. Very hard – it was in him to. Even when he wasn't under some truck, even at home he never stopped, around the house, outside. The soil we had! Clay and then just stony stuff on top. I know my father had tried to grow vegetables. But it wasn't a success. He'd given up by the time I came along. Neither of them were gardeners, really, not much. There was a lawn that always had daisies in it. Weedy you know? On the sunny side there were beds of those big red peonies you can see just coming up. There was a bright red rambling rose over a trellis – that's the wrong one, actually, but I'll keep looking. These two beds'll have carnations in them. Not well-behaved little pinks – big full-sized carnations that fall over and the plants'll get woodier and leggier year after year. The pansies you see now'll go on for most of the summer and they'll clash with the carnations *and* the peonies *and* the rose. I'll fill in some of the spaces with a sedum that's got tall feathery flowers later on. My mother called it Prince of Wales Feathers, which it isn't. Actually that's another plant entirely. As I said, they weren't gardeners. I'd guess most of it was stuff other people had passed on to them. I never remember them buying anything apart from the odd packet of seed for me. Oh and there'll be gaps – just brown earth between plants. Sunday afternoons my father would come out and hoe between the plants to stop them joining up. Very bad gardening form! Not the thing at all now.'

He moved his gaze this way and that as I pointed, nodding at the items that were already there and at the emptiness where others would be. And the emptiness that would never be filled. Quite suddenly I liked Nicky Kwok – really liked him and wanted health for him, wanted his going on into his own special future un-maimed and Nicky Kwok again. I imagined those hands beneath their wrappings, their moist centres caught and drying against the cotton. And the pull – the pain of that pull! The *agony* of it: any slight unthinking movement and the surface of the palm, so newly formed, is snatched away. Yet again.

'When I became a physician, my parents were very proud,' I told him. 'Though it meant I had no time for them. Then there was a time – after they were gone, thank God – when I drank too much. Hence not a doctor, now. I'm allowed to counsel. But you... your grandfather in particular is proud of you?'

'Yes.'

'Of course! You must be the perfect grandson. You're very brilliant, I hear.' There was no embarrassment: another slight dip of the chin. 'Yes! I have a perfect son myself to be proud of. His name's Jack. A brilliant son. As is his father, my husband – that was. I married the pick of the crop as they say. My husband, he got the best Maths first in the University. Bertrand Russell, you know, his was only the second best.'

We continued in quietness till the thrush returned almost to our feet, turning a skeletal last-year's leaf on the lawn and pausing to extract and devour a small grub. She disappeared over that questionable rambling rose to the ownerless plot.

'What does your grandfather grow?'

'Not many things. Around the pool house he tried to grow peaches but I think... too hot. They didn't do well. He has his persimmons still, but they're not good and... and...' He searched my garden with his eyes as he groped inwardly for a word, 'The beautiful white flowers – with smell?'

'Jasmine?'

'No. Bushes – in pots. Shiny leaves.'

'Um...'

'Gardenia!' he said with relief. 'Very many gardenias. He takes them in – out – tries them in different place, though the pots are big – very hard for him to move.'

'You miss him? Your family, all in Australia – but you miss him especially?'

'Yes.'

He looked away. I can only suppose it was something constitutional caused his sudden loss of control and allowed him to say what he said next....

These things, the things the Nicky Kwok's of this world present with, how can you define them? They're there in the text-book categories, but you might just as well let them form their own categories. Case histories *good*, theories *bad* – that was how I came to see it. Past tense. (Once I could've prescribed for him, and someone, when Steph could boost him far enough up the list, probably would do just that. Please, *please*, might he or she choose the least toxic in overdose). Whatever they are, these horrors, they arrive, they fester, they burst like boils. Here, side by side with him in my garden, nothing I did provoked his speech: I was under no misapprehension by now that Nicky Kwok felt deserving of remission for his bloody palms.

'He is eighty years old,' Nicky Kwok said, 'for my visit. Eighty. Three sons die before him in Kwangchow. His wife die. Only my mother, last child, left. He works. On boats, on the docks, then at buildings. Anything he must do. With wood, pieces of iron, bricks and stones....'

Only a need for breath caused him to stop. Not the raw meat around which he'd made fists. Though the book was far off and unrecoverable, a line from *Stigmata* came unsearched for into my mind: *A feature is the extraordinary precision of... conformity to the visualisation that triggered it.*

In this case the bricks, the stones, the wood tearing at an old man's hands. But there was more. It made me fear for

157

Nicky Kwok. 'Swearing at, made joke when...' he whispered, 'kicked out all teeth,' he laid his hand along his own lower jaw, fingers one side, thumb the other, seeming unaware of the red ooze he was anointing himself with. 'All gone. He works when he is child and then works at anything for seventy years. My mother and father bring him to Australia but.... Now he tries to grow persimmons and find place for gardenia bushes. Wrong place – they die.'

They die.

Had they died already – or was death for the gardenias a continual apprehension averted only by grandfatherly cunning, grandfatherly love?

'You could grow a gardenia,' I tell him. 'In a pot. I grew the peonies to start with. That's all they were, just some... things to start with. They're not instead of drinking, you get it? Though I don't drink – at present – and I do grow *them*.' But an unimpressive them, they were. Coarse bunches of leaves-in-waiting for the deep red hearts formed under and out of the dirt. 'With a gardenia,' I lectured him, 'you'll have to keep it in a pot. Bring it in, in the winter, for the cold months. I find it can be colder here than Wales. The Oxford winters can be harsh – pretty biting y'know?'

'Yes,' he said.

Almost an oxymoron: pretty biting. Biting, certainly. So hardy plants were my choice for harsh winters everywhere. The peonies... and Barb and Not-Barb's rose, they'd persisted.

We talked out the hour. I never saw him again. Did he...? I hope.

But that wasn't my final contact with Nicky. It was late September, summer's end. A drought. Jack's promised visit had failed at the last moment, leaving me vinegary with disappointment, unable to work or read or even eat the food I'd cooked on this, a close, Thames Valley evening that, finally, offered catharsis in a storm... but for someone else. From my kitchen window I watched the heavily laden clouds slip away to the south-west. I was scraping the slimy remains of pasta into the bin, taking especial interest in the trajectory of individual corn-coloured tubes, finding the movement disgusting, suggestive of... but I never pinned down suggestive of what. The phone rang: the mobile, still in the pocket I'd dropped it into, post Jack's cancellation. Two hours ago, it had been, and my heart leapt with the possibility that he was not at this exact moment speeding north by train, that the hours had folded back on themselves and here was Jack, in one second here was Jack's voice saying, 'OK, doc, just turning into the vineyard now have you ever thought how bad a deal you've given yourself – you, an alcoholic, living in a street called the vineyard...?'

There was no voice – at first. But a line had opened to some other place, though accidentally. (Rory still manages to do it all the time. Very rarely, Jack. Another little watering of hope). I could make out music, very piercing and pure: a flute, perhaps, or piccolo. The piper broke off too quickly for certainty – and then the background of rattling plates and cutlery came up and a tap's spurt. Somewhere in another kitchen a meal had just ended and one of the eaters cleared away while the other played snatches of a simple tune learned as a child. And then absolutely unmistakably I heard Nicky Kwok say, 'I like that one. Really good.' There came that high, Chinese laugh. 'I'll call now, yes? See if tonight.'

A hiss of annoyance was followed by disconnection.

I filled a tumbler at the sink and walked outside with it, sat beneath the cleared sky. Though dusty in its declining the garden was beautiful as a septuagenarian. The rose had overrun its trellis – rudely vigorous as Barb had threatened – the pansies were joined, brash mounds in betrayal of my father's dictum.

No gardenias for Nicky Kwok. But did he? I hope. I don't know.

Coo

Nothing dramatic.
Hardly original.
And not even particularly moving.
Not anything, really.
No trumpets. No Hallelujah Chorus.
And where was that beckoning light at the end of the tunnel?
Not there.
Just someone turning off a switch.

He'd read or heard (heard probably, he still couldn't stand books) what happens at times like these. When body and mind are fatally starved of oxygen and begin their downward spiral into blackness and decay, they do it in a strictly orderly fashion. (That's what she'd said, Professor Smartarse on one of those documentaries you find when you switch on and can't be bothered to get rid of). Breathing stops. Digestion ceases.

Motor functions fail. The liver gives up its long feud with the alcohol molecule, while saliva dribbles unswallowed across the chin. White cells float idly in the bloodstream – a bit like factory workers in a munitions plant downing tools while the air-raid threatens overhead. The heart is stilled. Vision contracts to a bright spot and then even this peep-hole on the world is lost.

It is the point of complete system failure.

And hearing remains.

So how come the would-be deceased finds it necessary to maintain it, this knack of identifying a pigeon's coo out on the window-ledge? This was something he wasn't going to get an answer to now. But for whatever the reason, the cooing of pigeons was the last thing his horribly abused brain registered as it went into its final shut-down...

...and the first as – against all the odds – it powered up for a brand new shift.

Coo-oo. Coo-hoo-oo.

Pigeons. Feral pigeons.

Into the no-colour world of closed eyelids a stray image of the sassy little cock-bird flashed: breast puffed out, the better to display the rainbow sheen of its feathers, circling before the chosen female, forever on the pull. Round and round it pattered, a beady gold-rimmed eye focused on whichever tatty hen was closest. He'd watched them, Saturday mornings, crossing the clubhouse car-park – and now, very distinctly, he could hear Noel Morgan's voice... Noel Morgan saying, 'Randy little tykes, pigeons are. Only bird in Britain breeds all year round. Always at it, hail, rain or shine. No wonder he looks totally shag...'

But Noel Morgan stopped in mid-sentence.

162

And the grey and buff and green dancing bird paused in its erotic revolutions and flickered and went out. And took him with it.

Funny that – well, not funny so much as interesting. Made you think. Like Professor Smartarse.

Noel Morgan – now there *was* a funny man. He could see him now, hanging over the rail of the ferry on the way back from Rosslare, heaving his guts into the Atlantic. The khaki waves coming at them are the size of hillocks. Noel's nursing a cracked rib. He's chucking up in well-advertised agony – and between heaves, he's telling them the one about the two nuns and the gorilla, 'And Sister Assumpta says, *Well of course it hurt!*' Heave-ho. '*Thirty years and he never...*'

Go on Noel. Finish the....

Noel Morgan didn't return, which was a pity because he had always liked Noel. Good old Noel – it was through Noel he'd first met... Paula, Paula of the tawny hair. Noel had been Paula's man of the moment until he'd cut in but that was OK because...

'Owain!'

A woman's voice. A woman was calling to someone.

'Owain?'

Something was tickling the back of his hand.

'I'm just here. It's me, again.'

Whatever it was, it was soft – annoying really – like a feather... like a pigeon's feather, or hair – more like hair – like the ends of a girl's hair, sweeping across his skin.

'Owain can you hear me? Can you? Go on – I know you can. I'll keep asking! Just having us on, aren't you? Eh, Owain. That's it, isn't it? Owain!'

It was a nice enough voice but – fuckitall – why couldn't this Owain bloke say something – anything would do, just to shut her up?

For an instant he opened his eyes. The glare, the horrible glare, forced a groan from... somewhere. He had no idea from where – and anyway he was slipping... backwards, ever backwards, his skull pounding, the fibres of his neck muscles threatening to fail and disjoin like old cables. The pain had him welcoming the blackness like a lover, even as she – she of the long tawny hair – said: 'It's me, Paula. It's me. I'm right here.'

'Right here,' she repeated – wherever here was.

And then, 'Coo...oo-hoo-oo-oo.'

Soppy cow.

That night – or day – he dreamed.

He was at the fun-fair, scooped up and hovering over the town – over the sea, now! – on a Big Wheel. On one side the breakers charged into the bay, on the other a girl in a flame-coloured dress hugged his arm, pressed her hip into his body, nuzzled her shining head into his neck. She 'Oh-ed' and 'Ah-ed' and filled his nostrils with a cheap, sweet perfume that blotted out the salt on the air and the hot oil of the engine that kept them revolving in space with only the sun above. Round and round, faster and faster. He had to stop it... had to...

'They're turning them!' Noel Morgan shouted... *from the touchline*. 'Llanelli's turning them.'

Knees and thighs straining, boots raking his calves: they needed to stop it. Just give him those few seconds to slither off the back of the scrum... just give him that single instant and he'd...

'The finest prop forward north Wales has ever...' said a smug and certain Oxbridge voice into one ear but the end was lost in a twenty-thousand-throat roar.

'The *only* prop forward north Wales has ever...' said the girl clothed in flame as the wheel dangled her, laughing and screaming, over the beach.

And then she must've got really scared because she started to cry. 'I'm sorry,' she said. 'Oh, thanks love. I usually bring some with me. Thanks.' She sniffed loudly – *didn't she get it? How even the slightest sound could cut through his head like a blade?* 'Shouldn't be doing this. I promised our Jonathan – no more of this.'

Jonathan.

It wasn't so much that he knew the name (not in the way that he knew Noel, say, or Paula) as that the name catapulted him straight out of himself and – where *now*? Where was this?

He was standing outside a huge building – three, four stories, Gothic turrets lost in the clouds. Towers and weird gravity-defying additions leaned out from every corner, broke every line of the massive Ffestiniog slates that were its roof. Rooks glided croaking across its grim façade – and at one tiny window a child's face was pressed against the glass.

'Jonathan!' a voice bellowed, his voice, 'I'm coming. I'll get you out!'

But he couldn't move. There were iron gates and a dank, paved courtyard to negotiate but no one blocking his path. Openings everywhere – yet there he stood, clasping the ball to his chest, cradling it like a woman soothing an infant... making no progress.

And there she was: Long Tawny Hair. It was falling across

165

his hands, his arms, and she was saying, 'Leave him! He's fine. Just 'cos you were rubbish at school, doesn't mean… you just leave Jonathan to me, eh?'

He tried to brush the hair away – it was tickling, it was holding him back but he couldn't do it. And the little figure disappeared from the window and he struggled until the tears ran down his own face in frustration and shame.

'Look, look! He's crying!' she said as though he needed showing up, when his son – that's who it was – his own son was trapped in there and here was he, nailed to the pitch, the sodden pitch that now surrounded him. All he had to do was drop that ball and slot it, sweet and true though those iron gate posts and…

Too late. The pack was upon him: the grass and the mud and the weight and the blackness. And then nothing at all.

Coo-coo-coo.

The pigeon was back.

He could hear it strutting its stuff, could picture its hopeful pink-footed shimmy.

Without thinking, he opened his eyes, flinching in preparation for… what? He couldn't remember now – something bad – but it didn't matter because whatever he feared left him unmolested this time. He was looking at a chintzy curtain hanging in a soft grey light. There was a *pattern*, on the curtain, but… it had a *pattern*, that curtain, but… the *pattern* on it… the pattern on the *curtain*… when he looked at a *piece* of that pattern it turned to fuzz.

Try again! Look at another bit.
Same thing.
'Owain!'

That voice – the woman's voice. And now a head came into view, a brilliant silk scarf across the forehead – orange and lemon silk burning in the failing light – and brilliant eyes, big dark eyes, staring into his own. He fought to get those eyes into focus, to look back.

'Owain!'

He felt his hand grasped – not tickled, this time, but grabbed and held and squeezed until the bones grated.

'Owain!'

Whoever Owain was, he didn't come – or not at first. The silken head bobbed out of sight and then reappeared. There was another beside it: boyish, olive skinned, smiling – dressed as... a dentist? 'Look, Ravi!' she turned and whispered to him. *Paula*, that was it. Miss Tawny Hair, under a scarf. 'He's awake,' she said.

Paula said.

'Mr Barry?' the boy asked.

So that's who he was. He was Mr Barry.

Against those bloody *poncy* curtains everything might be indistinct but inside his head he saw it all clearly: the red shirt stiffened with filth and sweat, but still matching the blood in the hand he wiped across his mouth... the woman holding up the child in the crowd... and the crowd chanting, louder and louder, 'Barry! Barry!'

He was Barry.

Barry was him.

So now he knew three – no, four people: Paula and Ravi and of course his son, Jonathan, who wasn't here now... and himself.

'Mr Barry? How are you? Do you know where you are? Do you know what happened, Mr Barry? You're in the Maelor

General. You're in hospital in Wrexham. You've been here –
Mr Barry?'

Why did the boy keep on like that, reciting his name?

Four people, he thought, and if this Owain-bloke ever
turns up, I'll know five.

Enough for a party.

Sleep – just sleep, that's all it was and waking... waking half-
way through something – something that involved his being
lifted and turned and a sharp but pleasant scent. It was
morning.

He knew it was morning.

He half-expected Ravi and Paula to be sitting there still.
Instead he saw two completely new characters.

Girls: one overweight and out of breath, the other with
plucked eyebrows and the face of a surprised doll.

'Back with us?' said Doll-Face.

'Hello, there, Owain,' said her partner. 'I'll tell Ravi, shall I?'

'Bar-ook,' he croaked. All three of them were shocked.

'Do they call you Barry? Is that it?' said the puffing one.

'No, he's trying to say Owain – aren't you Owain?' asked
Doll-Face.

'Bar-ook.' It was still the best he could do.

'There you are!' Doll-Face looked jubilant. 'Owain – clear
as a bell.... I'll, er, I'll tell Ravi, shall I?'

Ravi arrived to exorcise his confusion. 'Nice to see you
back Mr Barry. Bit of a shock, I think, for you. How are you
feeling?'

'Fi-oon,' he heard himself reply

Ravi smiled so all his beautiful white teeth were on show
at once. Nice to see a dentist looking after his own teeth. Good

advert. To Doll-Face he said, 'See if you can catch Mr Fenn-Jones, will you? If he's still on the ward. Oh and get someone to call Mrs Barry... yes?'

Softly, matily, out there on the ledge a pair of pigeons proclaimed their sexual bond.

Coo-coo-oo... hoo-oo!

'You've been here a month,' said Mrs Barry, who turned out to be Paula, Miss Long Tawny Hair – except, now that the scarf was gone, he could see the long tawny hair was cut into a neat geometric shape. This revealed, as she leant over him, garnet earrings and a pale, lined throat. The brown eyes were as big and warm as ever but surrounded by a map of wrinkles into which a sort of greasy gold eye make-up had settled.

'Do you remember anything – 'bout what happened, I mean?'

He shook his head. 'Oh-h. Shit.'

'No, I wouldn't do too much of that. You hit the post, you daft sod. Goin' back, you were, eye on the ball – fell and knocked yourself out! You don't know none of this, right?'

'Was it... rugby?' he suggested.

'Good God! I never thought I'd hear Owain Barry ask that. Was it rugby! Look, the doc's seen you has he?'

'I'm OK just a bit... hazy.'

'Well I'm not surprised. They carried you into the club-house and you weren't breathing. You died! A bit hazy? You could've been in a box.'

His eyelids closed of their own accord and he was aware of the weakness through his entire body and the dry-ash surface of his lips even though Doll-Face had given him a drink... several drinks. 'Jonathan'll be here,' she said with something extra in her voice, something he recognised and knew he'd missed. It was connection, concern. 'After school, of course.'

'You'll collect him... from the... school?' A terrible Gothic prison flashed up, its ribbon-pointing grim and clear. Like straps.

'Collect him? Why would I collect him?'

Old, familiar panic and frustration was tightening up his chest, had him turning, struggling onto his elbows, the vision of that lost and fragile face pressed to the glass, the black bodies of the rooks wheeling across the granite blocks, all the...

'Collect him! Lie down – shush now, *cariad*. He'll drive himself.'

'School,' was all he could manage, spat out like an expletive.

'Yes, that's right... Graig School – Owain? You know. Come on Owain, you do know. Jonathan – the school – he's head of Science? Youngest ever.'

His expression must've conveyed all those words and phrases, questions and demands that even now were trapped in a thick, moiling scrum on the back of his tongue. Paula pulled her plastic chair close and for the first time touched his cheek, stroked away the damp wisps from his forehead.

'You don't know, do you? Oh, poor Owain! But you know me, right?'

'Yes... but...'

How to explain?

A huge, fog-filled gulf seemed to separate him from the *now* he'd woken to.

'Your... um,' he pointed at the neat, swinging cut. 'It's... short... see your ears. I thought it was... down your back.'

'Oh-h,' she said, very slowly. 'Yes-s. I get it.'

170

She ran her splayed fingers through what was left of the long tawny hair and gave a nervous laugh. 'I'm off to get my roots done – later on. Celebrity dinner, tonight – something to do with The Round Table, isn't it? We're having Darren... um – you know? The snooker-player. God I've forgotten his name now.' She winked, her eyes shone and some quality to the instant caused his pulse to accelerate, his groin to tighten. 'It must be catching! Darren... anyway, a wonderful speaker, they say he is. *Rude*. Noel was lucky to get him.'

The still-brilliant eyes overflowed with tears. They turned the mascara into rivulets of coal-dust, the eye-shadow into a pinchbeck deposit across both cheek-bones. He'd seen this before. This he remembered. The strange room made out of unfathomable fabric, the narrow metal bed... the bowl with its tangerines withered to the size of pigeons' eggs... and the bloody ever-cooing pigeons themselves, out there beyond the dirty glass – all these were a mirage, surely, the debris of some event not understood or not meant to happen? But the tears. They were true. They were real.

He reached out a hand lapped by an unfamiliar blue sleeve but she didn't take it and when he looked at the rejected hand – his hand – there was a long, ragged scar running from below the thumb, round and across, almost to the wrist-bone. Nasty, it looked, but it was an old injury, an old, deep incision, curved as a short drop goal. You couldn't help but follow it – with the eye, with the mind. Nodules of purple scarring had formed, he saw, half-obliterating those lines along the inner arm that were tracks of veins or arteries... a vein or an artery? One made its way towards the heart and one came back. He wasn't sure how to distinguish which was which – but he didn't think he'd ever been able to.

171

Very nasty. That must've hurt... once.

'You remember Noel, yeah? I went off with him twenty years ago, Owain. I couldn't stand all your... just couldn't say no, could you? Just couldn't ever, one single time in your whole sodding life say... oh, *what does it matter*?' The tears had evaporated as quickly as they'd sprung, he saw. A dry season was come upon her, the crow's feet left like faults in a rock face but with nothing to course down them now. She back-handed her own cheeks making the wreck worse. 'Never asked me to marry him, didn't Noel – but then *I* never asked *him*, neither. It's stupid, though, the name thing... and here, you know...' she gestured to somewhere he had no knowledge of, somewhere beyond the chintz. 'They go and assume, don't they? Anyway we're happy enough, me and Noel – and we've got the girls. *And* he's been like a father to Jonathan....' Angrily she shook her head and the garnets flashed. 'They only rang me in the first place because our Jon was away on a school trip – and you've got nobody else.'

She jumped to her feet in agitation, became entangled in the curtain and rounded on him as she fought it off. 'I shouldn't really be here. It's not Mrs Barry, it's Paula Barry. I'm not your wife. I'm nothing... we're nothing now...'

'How old?' he asked.

'Me? Or you? Doesn't matter, does it? We're both fifty-four.'

He swallowed, just the once, but so hard he heard his own gullet contract. And then he grinned.

'Still playing though, eh?'

'No you're not, you silly old.... Ach! *Charity Shield*! And you were the referee.'

Auntie Shar's Seasoning

The Graig Women's House is grey as the outside street – but within everything that paint and enthusiasm could do has been done. The narrow hall glows hot pink to leave no one of the wrong gender in any doubt as to the clientele it wishes to welcome and empower. The small meeting room? A lime green to suggest 'growth through conflict resolution'. The kitchen has been stippled in a deep ox-blood overlaid with tomato, presumably to discourage an undesirable obsession with hygiene. The ceilings throughout the building are low and beamed and tend towards the oppressive however they are coated in a brilliant yellow gloss...

So it was that on a wet morning in September when Hester Lloyd nee de Quela walked into reception, she seemed to have come home. Out in the stone-and-slate town her emerald silk jacket and gold trousers outshone the traffic lights but here they settled into the rainbow colour card of the background, perfectly.

Gwen Porrett heard the bell, poked her head around the glass partition, recognised the visitor and experienced a deep and satisfying warmth. At last. Hester de Quela had come to them, just as they had hoped... had *known* she must.

For a second or two Hester was unaware she was observed. She stalled, uncertain as a faun... and when a coil of her hair touched the low, paper lampshade she crouched and backed away. Her tiny, coffee-coloured hands clutched at the green edge of her jacket. Her arched brows rose still further, in what Gwen took to be alarm. Before this exquisite creature bolted Gwen decided she had better make herself known.

'It was a present, the lampshade, from the Association of Women's Communes of Caracas. It's never really worked for me.'

Hester turned to her. 'But a kind thought.' Close to she was even tinier, making Gwen, who was not exactly tall herself, feel Amazonian.

'Yes! You're right. But knitting's more their thing. They sent us all a poncho each, one year. 'Course no one would wear them and now, would you believe it, they're back in fashion? So – how are you? I'm Gwen and welcome to The Graig Women's House – which, as you can see, is, er, us...'

'Or why would you have the sign on the door?' the visitor chipped in unexpectedly.

'Er, yes. Right again. Well, I'm Gwen, as I said, just a volunteer. We're all just volunteers. And you....' Gwen realised that this was not a sentence she could easily complete. Of course, she knew Hester de Quela (she couldn't bring herself to use the demeaning name of Lloyd even in her thoughts). Everyone in the entire town knew that in early summer Howie Lloyd – a fat, fifty-something insurance salesman... balding, boorish, Howie Lloyd – had taken the second of two holidays to Goa, and brought back a wife... except that no one in Graig called her a wife. The first Mrs Lloyd (whose only distinguishing feature in urban legend was that she'd once visited family in Newport and never returned) – now *she* had been a wife.

Hester de Quela was a *mail-order bride*.

Gwen's husband Paul had pointed out – with typical pedantry – that strictly speaking she could not be mail-order, Howie having had to make the trip out there to collect his prize. It did nothing to detract from the established, hateful concept in The Graig Women's House. Sightings of the MOB were reported at weekly meetings. Encounters with Howie were also mentioned by male partners: Howie sounding very pleased with himself, Howie losing a bit of weight by the looks of it. Howie lapsed from the cricket club, not available for the darts team.

Gwen, Susan, Liz, Di and Wyn watched and waited.

'I was wondering about help,' Hester began. Her English certainly was very good, precise and with just a touch of the exotic to add to its surprisingly throaty charm.

'Of course, love.' Gwen laid a protective hand on the visitor's arm and encouraged her to sit. The rumour was 'twenty-two, twenty-three tops,' and surely she could be no more? Perhaps she could. Her heart-shaped face was pretty rather than beautiful, her eyes as big as a marmoset's. But an intelligent marmoset. A marmoset that knew its way around the forest. 'Plonk yourself down there, I'll get us some tea and we can have a bit of a chat. You drink tea, don't you?' Hester rewarded her with an enigmatic smile – it might have been shyness... or something else entirely... 'Er, fine then.'

175

Hester did drink tea though the *THINK GLOBAL – ACT LOCAL!* mug looked out-size in her childish grip. 'My name is Hester Lloyd, I...'

'Married Howie.'

'Howell, yes. I come originally from a part of India called...'

'Goa. I know. Susan's Gareth runs the travel agent. We got the brochures... and then the library ordered us *The Rough Guide*. *Hester*, yeah? That'll be a hangover from the Portuguese. Though from the looks of the photos you're letting some of those old Catholic churches go. Not that we can talk. The chapel sells carpet roll-ends now... I'm sorry, love,' Gwen faltered. Hester's impassive features forced her to reconsider: she'd been unwise to raise the subject. Eastern people were naturally spiritual whereas for herself... religion was like so many other Big Things – cloning, the arms' trade, the menopause – the more you thought about it, the more miserable it made you. 'I don't know why I'm running on like.... What can we do for you? But let me say this straightaway, there's a room upstairs is yours this minute, no questions asked. And we've the Rescue Fund – won't take you back to Goa but it'll get you to just the other side of St Asaph. There's a proper refuge there and it'll give us time to take stock.'

For an instant Gwen feared she'd progressed too quickly and that Hester would clam up. Secretly – she had to admit it – she'd been anticipating this moment, this roll-call of Howie's iniquities... and it brought a tightness to her throat to see the younger woman pressing what looked like a charm, a little wizened monkey made out of – plastic, was it? Over and over in her delicate fingers it tumbled as if it were a favourite toy.

'I think,' Hester said, 'if you don't mind, we should have another cup of tea.'

'She said *what*?'

Gwen had known the sort of response she might expect. 'She said that she owed Howie a debt. For not charging 'dear Auntie Sharmilla' a penny – for taking her off Auntie's hands.'

Paul was so struck with the idea he turned away from the compelling spectacle of two identical racing cars going round and round a series of bends. 'Yes, that's right,' Gwen said bitterly, 'in Goa even a useless lump of humanity like Howie Lloyd can expect to be paid to marry a girl like Hester. A business arrangement. It's called a dowry.'

'I wonder how much I could have got for...'

'Don't even think it!'

Paul's eyes drifted back to the screen. As far as Gwen could make out nothing much had happened except the blue car and the mainly-white car had changed position. Paul sighed – but then grinned good-naturedly. 'So what's she doing at Coven Central, then?'

'Wants to help out, playgroup, housebound visiting... bless her.'

Nothing, not even the precocious, dank, Welsh autumn could diminish Hester. Howie, to general amazement, drove her all the way over to Manchester one Saturday where she picked out the finest cashmere coat The Graig Women's House had ever seen. Gwen, Susan, Di and Wyn (though with Wyn it was only just) took turns modelling it up and down the kitchen. 'Beautiful,' Gwen enthused to Paul, 'and so light, you hardly know you've got it on – except you're warm.' Beneath the

177

navy coat Hester still shimmered in her coloured silks and embroidered jackets, her scarves sewn with silver beads and bells... but if Hester remained the bright little peacock of her arrival, something was happening to Howie that caused old acquaintances to stop in the street and stare after him: that caused a sudden quietening at the bar, on his rare approach.

Howie – whose arrival anywhere had for years been preceded by his personal tribute to the lager-maker's art – was now half the man. Estimates of the loss ranged between three and four stone... and starvation was not the key. Hester proved a wonderful cook for, it seemed, Auntie Sharmilla ran a tourist café. A veritable little gold mine, although no more than a Goan beach-hut, its food was famous from Stockholm to Sydney. And her niece had been thoroughly trained. Fridays she'd cook *bangra with caja* for lunch at The Women's House (although the *bangra* was still swimming in the Indian Ocean, mackerel did just as well). On the morning Hester announced that 'the meal will be easy today, friends. Howell ground all the cashews last night to save me the trouble,' Gwen feared there might be a fatality through shock in the blood-red kitchen.

'Perhaps she's wearing him out,' was Paul's suggestion. 'I mean, what are we looking at – a fifteen year drought since the last Mrs Howie...?'

'Don't!' Gwen found it impossible to imagine Hester naked; this was the girl who had draped Gaynor Pugh with tea-towels when those Christmas-fig nipples had popped out for her twins. Not naked, not Hester. Instead, she saw the gold silk trousers encompass a pink recumbent Howie – as the little silver scarf bells tinkled rhythmically.

Tinkle, tinkle, tinkle.

'Some things,' said Gwen, 'it's best not to think about. What that lovely girl gets up to with Howie Lloyd is top of my list.'

Tinkle, tinkle.

'In fact it's all of my list.'

'Well whatever's doing it, it's making his hair grow,' Paul acknowledged – it was part grumble, part salaam... and it was true. Everyone had noticed how Howie was no longer shaving his head – that forlorn attempt to ape Sir Anthony Hopkins that fooled nobody. The re-growth was scalp-wide and sandy. 'And he's been promoted... no more living off commission. Office manager. The word is, he's coining it.' He returned his attention to his rapidly emptying plate. 'What d'you say this was?'

'Fish curry. There was some left over and...'

'Mm-mm. Eat up, then. I thought we might,' he nodded, allusively, toward the ceiling, 'you know...'

Gwen stared, speechless, at the dining room clock. It was all of ten past seven.

And 'D'you know what?' Di had said only the day before, dropping into a precautionary whisper lest Hester appear. 'I bumped into Howie in the Post Office – letters to Goa. Talk about makeovers – let me go ahead of him in the queue! If you didn't know who it was... and what he used to be like, you could almost....' *What* you could almost was lost in shrieks of laughter.

Posters for 'The Spices of Goa in Cooking and Healing – An Illustrated Talk' went up in the library and clinic at the start of the New Year. The promise of news from the tropics had an audience of twenty braving the horizontal sleet and packing the biggest room in The Women's House. Hester, composed and smiling, stood before them. The famous cashmere coat had fallen away to reveal a new outfit of finely-worked scarlet tunic and tailored black trousers, a fusion of styles. No scarf, no silver bells, no mirror-work: nothing to distract the eye from the sharp outline of her faultless proportions against the spiritual-blue paint of the Meditation and Sharing Space. Hester's only prop lay on the table: a small, dark wood box – more pygmy chest of drawers, really – whose compartments and hidey-holes she was busily unpacking. 'My friends,' she began, 'today I wish to share with you, here in your Women's House, a gift... something from your sisters in Goa, some*things* of practical use, in return for the kindness of Graig.'

The gift certainly seemed modest. A dozen or so muslin bags, each no bigger than a book of stamps... then came a few small trinkets, carved animals, in a dirty-green mineral or of bone. But when the neck of each little sachet was opened and the mini-zoo lined up, a wonderful aroma filled the room. Women could be seen breathing deeply through flared nostrils – one or two loosened winter woollies, unbuttoned jackets... and to everyone's relief, Gaynor Pugh's twins dropped off to sleep.

'This box contains my dowry – all that she could give me, my dear Auntie Shar, who was not even my aunt, but who took me in when I was no older than those babies and my parents dead... and I wasn't the only girl she had rescued – and... *educated*. Now, I am afraid I have a confession to make to you all,' here even Wyn – who'd been overcome by the orphan prologue and begun sniffing – looked up sharply. 'I have no lecture to give. In Goa we pay our debts. Howell married a girl with neither family nor money – and despite what many of you must think, he'll be a good husband – and I will be a good wife.' For some reason this phrase provoked muttering in the back. The speaker pressed on. 'But the company of women is most important in whatever part of the world you find yourself. As Auntie Shar would tell you if she were here, men in every land live like goats – it is with the goatherds that wisdom lies.'

Hester had the knack of pleasing, Gwen thought, as the grins spread across face after face.

And that was it. For every woman there was a confidential word (Gwen caught *Now Susan, you'll find Gareth's trouble easily remedied*)... and a small measure of one spice or another was tapped out and offered in a twist of paper. For some a carved figure was slipped into the hand by Hester and held tight enough for its silhouette to be left in the palm's skin like a stamp. Gwen found herself impressed with the sign of the tortoise. ('Well you did say your neck was going,' Liz pointed out.) There were also a few strands of something seedy and withered – to be put into soup.

'I should do this because...?' Gwen asked.

'To remind *you*,' Hester said, 'that your children have gone out into the world healthy and happy, and Paul still loves you after nearly thirty years.'

It was true.

She hadn't thought of it in so many words for a long, long time but it *was* true. 'I don't need to be told that,' Gwen said stiffly.

'Not now,' Hester said.

'I mean I don't need... magic to remind me.'

'But Gwen, of course you don't. And anyway *magic* – as you call it – like friendship, like love, like marriage... it's all just good business in the end.'

Morfa

'Star of Bethlehem' it had been called, the missing cottage. On a day like this it was easy for him to see how it might have been simply washed away. *The rain*. Although over for the present, the traffic out on the Chester road passed with an accompanying, persistent hiss. Slates' run-off gurgled away in the downspouts as though someone had left a tap on... which, in one sense and if you believed that sort of thing, He had. The wettest year on record for Flintshire – no, no longer for Flintshire anymore, for the whole of north Wales.

Rosa, ever the Londoner, pointed out: 'and that must've been up against some pretty damn hot opposition.'

'Pretty damn hot' – two generations out of Emilia-Romagna and its rhythms came across still as her full lips fondled each sound. Pret-ty damn hot. She smiled as she said it: a four-syllable curse. You couldn't blame her – hardly her idea to maroon them both in *his* shabby bit of the country.

Their third move in five years. Not her way, either, to moan. He'd seen so many partners of physicians, male and female alike, take up the hobby when twitched from job to job: career building, a three-legged race where the reluctance of either contestant threatened a tumble. Not Rosa, though. Find work, replace the friends – it was what you could do if you had the knack.

Buy a smart new house.

The village he'd left had swollen in his absence. The terraces and council-owned semis were circled by modern villas now – and, post-Battersea, to him and Rosa ('We're Opfinks, *caro* – did you know that? One point five incomes, no kids!') embarrassingly cheap ones. And they'd never known such space; big square rooms that hadn't been converted into this, trimmed to fit in that. Their minimal furniture fled to the corners leaving empty expanses of gleaming wood. For the first time since qualifying, he felt – *they were* – in the money. But outside one more Vaseline-grey dawn followed the next. Beyond the table where they snatched breakfast there lurked a vista over which the weather always had the upper hand; it squatted, huge and immovable, on the too-close horizon. At these smeared, eight o'clock showings what was a homecoming for him must seem to Rosa like a posting to the edge. *Must* because she wasn't saying.

And to keep on not saying for nearly a year – no, for the wettest year on record. Surely that meant the curse was *his* invention? Pret-ty damn hot. A joke, that's all. They never argued. 'The rain's what forms the landscape,' he'd suggested, gently... and 'I've always had this thing about it – hated it when Mum and Dad moved away. I never want to live far from the sea again. The Saltney Marsh and the Dee estuary – the Welsh call it *morfa* – it defeated the Romans.'

184

'Excuse my lack of surprise. But I won't take it personally.'
And once he said, 'The name for Earth should be Ocean.'
...would have explained if she'd asked him to.

Just as with Star of Bethlehem, the lost cottage. He would
have explained – or would have tried.

Next to the window of the dull box that was his consulting
room hung a painting. The right-angles of its frame were no
longer true. Against *The Ear, Inner Ear and Eustachian Tube*
(provided by some drugs firm in red, blue and green) its
pigments were feeble. Offered for a tenner at a car-boot sale,
Rosa was never going to give it wall space.

'Ten pounds? We don't collect junk,' she'd said over her
shoulder. Her theory was that a single, decent item lurked
somewhere in every Sunday market – and having found it, you
left. She had an excellent eye. In this case she'd homed in on
the treen apple, despite its layers of grime; now it was
wrapped in newsprint, Rosa was ready for lunch. 'I thought
that place at Erbistock? The Boat?' And when he'd brought
out *his* buy over the linguine (at that place at Erbistock – The
Boat) she'd greeted it with a scornful smile.

Today, he let his gaze rest on the tatty little embellishment,
between patients – telling himself it was good for relaxing the
ciliary muscles... keeping at bay that new ache across the temples until...

No – not 'We don't collect junk.' That wasn't right. It was
'*I* don't collect junk.' That's what she'd said.

Junk.

He didn't see junk. He saw an ink-and-watercolour of a
cottage... almost a child's idea of home: a dark front door,
crossed glazing bars of one adjacent window and just tiny
black rectangles let into the upper storey for the others. The

185

lone, slim chimney stack pointed at three birds (turtle-doves perhaps?) sweeping over the thatched roof. Trees clustered up against the building with a mateyness that would've had any modern householder scanning his foundations for cracks, his insurance policy for fine print. A low picket fence cordoned off what might have been a bit of domestic horticulture from the wild, waste ground surrounding it.

Inside the glass, up against the mount, someone had stuck a handwritten label, yellowed and faded and blotched with the same degree of foxing that marred both the mount and the painting itself. It read: 'This is an artist's recollection of a shepherd's cottage which once stood at the end of what is now North Street, Saltney Ferry. It bore the name "Star of Bethlehem", and the artist is believed to be J G Brown.'

'Star of Bethlehem'.

Perhaps it was simply the cryptic nature of its name that drew him.

He'd take the long way round from surgery to home just to pass where it had stood: an outpost of the unaccommodated past.

He could never turn into Saltney Ferry Lane without thinking of that single, flickering lamp. It would've shone out across the boggy flats of Saltney Marsh, which might have had a new English name by then, but were still *Morfa Caer Leon*... two thousand acres of legion-defying swamp. How welcome to a traveller, floundering and lost in the khaki fractal of its dusk. The cottage, swept and warm, the snug reed-thatch, yearly renewed, shelter for man and dove... and the picket fence, tarred and upright, a clean edge with the moist uncertainties of the outside. Best of all would have been the light sparkling on the window's four panes.

The Star.

For a while it held a fascination, as the unlikeliest things had the power to do, especially lately. A new maze in which his sore, disappointed self could get lost. He must know, must find out.

'What?' Rosa had demanded. There was always a rise at the corners of those rounded lips, an invitation to lighten the tone. Back in the hospital's miasma, where they'd met, this instinct for humour had attracted him powerfully. Even now, even as he suspected he was so often its butt, he found it irresistible. 'Come on, Dr Sad! What can there possibly be to find out?'

He had no reply and shook his head and smiled back as though she'd won the point. But a stolen couple of hours he'd used in taking the trip into nearby Hawarden, driving up the long hill from Broughton, *out* of the marsh. Half of the population of the county seemed to have had the same, spur of the moment idea: the narrow main street was blued with exhaust fumes, thickening and souring the moist air. Parked illegally in front the Gladstones' mock-Gothic pile, he dodged across into the Record Office.

'*Now* – did you know that Saltney's the only village in Britain that straddles a national boundary? People always think half-and-half, but it isn't – Welsh side's bigger by... o-oh a fair bit, anyway that's not to say a lot of Saltney people don't get more joy over on the English side. Chester families will have moved across and back and so on, over the years. It is family history, is it?'

'No, no, it's just general interest...' but the woman had turned to someone following him in. As with Rosa there was no need for real explanation....

He crouched at his allotted work-station, the books piled defensively around him, the maps – ordered from some secret stash – oversized and turning unruly when spread. He had always known there was strangeness loose in the place: Saltney meant simply *salt marsh* – a warning rather than a settlement. As a child there was the constant interest of the sluices opening and closing, the lane that could flood without explanation on a dry day. No one, not his parents nor any adult, mentioned this enigma – although an old woman, a neighbour, had scared him sleepless with a tale of her girlhood. It was a tale of the embankment's only failure: how the river Dee had topped it, inundated the boat yards and the little workshops and, finally, the stinking renderers and come roaring through the darkened streets. It had floated the pews out of St Matthews, the barrels out of The Prince of Wales and The Corner Pin – and before the wave ran a living carpet of rats. *'These commons called Saltney were anciently covered by the sea,'* Thomas Brock, a self-appointed chronicler, had written in 1777, *'and in perpetual danger of being destroyed by the flux and reflux of the tide....'*

A whole village – over two thousand people now – buoyed up on a barely-wrung-out sponge! Although old and shoddy-seeming to Rosa, a couple of hundred years ago Saltney had not been there – because there was no there. For some reason it thrilled him to imagine the cold and antiseptic sea sweetening the channels and pools twice daily... washing over Lavenders' garage where they serviced his car, rising to the flat roof of the pine furniture factory, inundating each equinox the ugliness of the Saltney Ferry Hotel. (*'...and the eleventh of this month is remarkable for a horse being swallowed up on the New Road and afterwards drawn up by ropes, quite dead'*).

188

It could still take back – with violence – its stolen demesne. Thomas Brock... how reliable a source was he?... hating the marsh as they all hated the untouched, the un-befouled leys and winding creeks... wanting to possess what had once been common. *A fallible narrator*: the phrase, straight out of the Sunday supplements, might have been coined for the man. And the partial narrative? If its missing elements were the product of artistry, ignorance or avarice, it had still proved viable. All Brock need do was, in the great tradition of story-telling, make a villain of his victim... it became the hunchback with its swelling green islands, the lascivious duchess creeping into every forbidden cranny, the thief....

Now the archives revealed an unexpected and ruthless menu of progress: the wilderness was first incised by Nathaniel Kinderley's Saltney Cut – nine miles of handcrafted canal. But this was no ordinary canal. This feat of navigation must contain a volatile river intent on losing itself in swamp. The arrogance of the man, Kinderley, to take it on, armed with nothing but the muscle-power of the poor. But somehow the Dee was captured, the vast acreage snatched and enclosed – and then the pastoral replaced by the profitable. '*These...*' what was it?

'*These commons called Saltney*' – the very term betrayed the place. Common – 'open or free to all' on the following line becomes 'vulgar and inferior'. No more than a matter of usage, a stroke of the pen, the demonised marsh was portioned out, given away. Though Brock took his share, it was the aristocratic Glynne family, ever hungry for land, who grabbed most. It was they had constructed the causeway from which men and horses still strayed to a glutinous end ('*if you turn your eyes on Saltney Marsh you will see carriages or at least as much of them as the horses have been obliged to leave behind with the load sticking immoveable for days'*). But with the cutting of a canal, the embarrassment of water could at last be poured into somebody's pocket. (The name for Earth should be Ocean, he'd thought, as he scribbled away the few pencilled notes which within the week he'd find himself crumpling and throwing on top of the used gloves and tongue depressors.)

'Star of Bethlehem' foundered as his attention raced through the early decades of a community that had sprung from nowhere. The marsh, a wasteland of water and mud, was suddenly alive with surnames still represented on his patient list. English, Welsh and Irish had flowed in: Prices, McBrides and Talbots.

In the nineteen-hundreds the railway arrived to muscle out the slate traffic from the river-wharf. Still-new villages of Saltney and Saltney Ferry oozed imperceptibly into one another. The Great Western company drained even more land as best they could, built an engine shed and a barracks and soon there was a school and a chapel to serve two new streets off Saltney Ferry Lane. These were North and Ewart – forever damp, red-brick terraces of shunters and wheel-tappers and their families.

Why not North and South Street? Too easy?

Why not Ewart and Gladstone Street? William Ewart Gladstone had become the local bigwig by then, successor to the Glynnes.

Nobody left alive remembered. But on the map of 1909 (another purchase to break up that dull, consulting-room wall) 'Star of Bethlehem' was gone.

The call put afternoon surgery into welcome remission.

'Got to go, Nev.'

'Right – bad news for some poor sod, is it?' Nev, for whom the drudgery of general practice retained nil interest these days, found these occasional police call-outs maddening. Perhaps because he'd given up the offer himself? An emaciated patient seated shirtless and shivering on Nev's examination table was ignored.

'Suspicious death, is it?'

'No idea, sorry,' he lied.

The address came as no surprise: twenty-two, North Street. He knew the residents of North Street and Ewart Street and Saltney Ferry Lane as frequent, multi-troublesome customers. Given time, he might have been able to come up with a complete medical history for this one...

Except that it would be useless now.

There was always something squalid, he thought, about a dead body inside a house. In the open air, sprawled in a ditch, half-buried in the forest – that was almost natural. A landscape feature. Young people dying in an act of violence, the soil an accommodating sump for fluids – or oldies, slipping forward after that faltering, last-ever step, all strength consumed: it was where human beings had died for thousands – no, hundreds of thousands of years.

But this – this was just too contrived.

The woman lay loosely curled against an overturned chair, a carmine arrangement of legs, straggling dark hair, cheap fabric shoes, denim dress and open hands. Odd that they were not clutched to her throat in that hopeless attempt he's seen once before to keep life in. She'd bled out where she fell. Only a pair of resentful grey eyes suggested a late inkling of her own predicament... when he followed their gaze, he found her last take on existence must have comprised a low

191

grimy coffee table with its Diet Pepsi can, Bacardi bottle, overflowing ash-tray, soiled tissues – and a greasy, framed photograph of a giant, pink baby. Dust and filth everywhere. He stood up and backed away, careful of where he placed each paper-clad foot. There were already too many fresh and drying mud-prints on the carpet. They brought back a day, not so very long ago... Rosa walking straight in off the lawn, the emerald slivers falling from her dagger-heels, the daisies left to wither on the wooden boards...

Out.

He needed to get out.

'There's what looks like blood all over the kitchen floor,' Danny Radnor told him. 'No sign of SOCO yet, surprise-fuckin'-surprise! – oh, and it's on the walls and ceiling.'

'Ceiling?'

'Yeah, I know – a spurter. What d'you think?'

The convenient angle of the woman's chin allowed him to point without moving.

'One wound – very deep. If it's self-inflicted – this *isn't* self – it's usually more than one, yes? They have a trial go at it. But we have a single cut. There's trauma to the larynx – probably. *Rapid* exsanguination. That's bleeding to you, inspector.'

'Yeah, yeah,' Danny said.

'Somebody – he – cut her throat next door. She dragged herself in here?'

'That's what I'd guess.'

'I'll go see if you like. I've done the liver. She's not down to room temperature, by the way, and there's rigor still present. You know you should have a path-boy out here?'

Danny's way was to ignore censure. 'So... not *quite* fresh.... And, yeah, when they get us another I'll use him – or her.'

192

There was no rebuttal for that. 'Well, a little party last night, by the looks of things.' He hated himself for the appeasing tone. 'Anyone see her alive and well and chatting to the milkman?'

'Nope.'

'There you go, then. Things usually get nasty in the early hours.'

'Been at some women's refuge in St Asaph. *Came back* – now that was a good idea. Raised voices and screams around two-thirty this morning, say next door.'

'I must be psychic.' He glanced at the new watch Rosa had given him for their anniversary – very slim, very stylish but with an indistinct dial. 'Death confirmed at... four o'clock.'

'Tea time!'

'What?'

Sheepishly the policeman looked down at his gloved hands and grinned. 'Nothing to fuckin' eat – Freudian slip. Come on – don't give me that! Tomorrow one of your lot'll be presenting me with the complete stomach contents in a dish.'

'And you don't have any?'

Danny patted the muscular corrugations visible even through a winter-weight shirt. 'Correct.'

'Good time to get rid of you, then. I could pop you somewhere warm, go and give a talk on forensic medicine to the WI. And emerge with a perfect alibi. Time of death? Three hours later than I'd done the deed. And I'd have a roomful of respectable ladies – the sort that own hats – to keep me out of jail.'

Slowly, almost teasingly, he peeled the soiled latex from his fingers and dropped it into a plastic bag. The photographer was a new, impossibly youthful little creature, her curly head

193

bright with raindrops. He watched her with a desperate pleasure that was completely asexual for she held around her, as though in a bubble, a whiff of the clean after-rain air, the unused elements. He tried a smile. She almost elbowed him aside in her eagerness to get at the body, to prove to the two males in the room that she was hard as the tiled Art Deco hearth where the victim's glasses lay.

'And how would you do it? Get rid of me,' Danny probed.

'People always ask me that, for some reason... always ask doctors.'

'Go on. How would you?'

'Oh,' he was squeezing past, towards the door – as though to give Ms Snap-Happy more angles, more space. 'You'd have tripped.' He shrugged. 'And all he had to do was grab her by the raven locks and bash her forehead against that...' both Danny and the girl followed his gesture to the wicked-looking edge of the mantelpiece, 'and so would she. Who's to know?'

'Shit,' Danny's bland expression was a study in smooth tanned flesh-tones, 'remind me to watch my back with you.'

'How is it, by the way?'

'What?'

'Your back.'

'Oh – yeah. Good. Much better.'

'Told you Rosie'd sort you out.'

But Danny had turned his complaining back and led the way to the kitchen muttering self-consciously about the murder scene – this, presumably, for the benefit of the girl.

'Get a look at this lot. Right mess, eh?'

Blood thrown like paint up the wall by the elderly cooker... blood already dried on the faux-marble worktop... blood decorating the earthenware plates, the half-consumed loaf... blood floating in scarlet skeins on the surface of a spilt pool of vegetable oil.

Out.

He had to get out.

There were still sandbags propped against doorsteps, suggestive of the local, innate pessimism. 'The wettest year on record...' as though any record could stretch back to the forming of this, God's palm-print on the border of Wales.

He made his way under the festive police cordon ('Hello Craig – you kept the eye, then!' 'No thanks to you, doc.') and over to a car that screamed Official Stranger On Call in this area. Chip-paper had blown and caught under the Volvo's front wheel. The skinny cat nosing it slunk away. A small crowd of neighbours (various ages, both sexes, children well-represented) was starting to gather in North Street across from the dead woman's front door. Their solemn faces turned to the vehicle as he cruised around them and one – familiar in its seediness, a patient presumably – mouthed a question which the engine drowned out. Without thinking, he headed in the direction of the river. There was a spot by the footbridge – an unclassified, bald bit of soil and chippings, somewhere to conclude private transactions. Here you could pull off the road. Here, just beyond the derelict chapel, the village failed. Sky was the thing, as it was over any flat landscape... sky with its wide possibilities (when the murk shifted) for a brilliant white display, a fresh beginning even at the day's departure.

While the ordered, spotless car interior held him safe and apart he could survey the huge fields that the Saltney Cut had released. They were for vegetable growing and in this season it was a sombre crop. Blue green acres – autumnal sprouts – stretched in straight lines to the vanishing point. Closer to, the Cut itself (despite its playful, fatal currents) this late afternoon showed a surface of polished pewter with porcelain knick-knacks of gulls....

A terrible anger took him, a physical thing, easy to diagnose in the soaring pulse-rate and the acid bubbling up into a dry mouth. *Anger*: the dead woman was at its heart (but not its cause) *and* whoever had killed her – *and* the child that he couldn't bring himself to ask about. What a lame-brained idea had it been to come back here – to expect Rosa to see it as he saw it, to find content in its familiar ugliness?

'I don't collect junk,' she'd said.

And, 'What? Find out what?'

Why 'Star of Bethlehem', perhaps... and who had lived there and kept a single light shining out across the desolate emulsion of blue clay and the Dee.

(*'Whilst the marsh was not entirely uninhabited or without pathways it appears to have been a dreary and dangerous place. Parish records testify to the many tragedies – deaths by drowning or murder....'*)

Mary she'd been called, according to Danny Radnor. Mary Talbot, just late of twenty-two North Street... the end of North Street, where 'Star of Bethlehem' had once been fashioned out of the marsh itself. Mary... 'I'd be all right if it wasn't for the *stuff* – nasty 'e gets on it. Not just smokin' it anymore, see. We used to laugh! Couldn't wait for the kids to finish their chocolate so 'e could get hold of the silver paper for 'is smoke.' (Was that a true memory or a composite of other troubles, other supplicants?)

Not just smokin' it anymore, see.

196

Mary call the cattle home across the sands of Dee.

Poetic licence for mainly mud – just a matter of usage.

In a moment he would get out. Not now but soon. Ever since his foray into research, the weirdness of Saltney seemed to have got under his feet. There were days – today was definitely one of them – when he could *feel* the give of the ground. He'd walk on the sodden grass, each step compression and resurgence – then, paper covers notwithstanding, he'd examine his shoes one more time. It'd be good to breathe in that distant promise of the sea, renewed with every tide – while only a mile away good old Nev worked through an extended list of insomnia, mood swings, chronic fatigue... and vague pains in the region of the heart.

Propped against the dashboard the handsome features of Danny Radnor observed him from a faded plastic card. THE DEE VIEW HEALTH AND FITNESS CLUB, it read, MEMBERSHIP No: 0105. There was still a gritty deposit overlaying it, from its hiding place up against the skirting that ran behind his side of the bed. And removing the card had left a clear silhouette. He could see it now with absolute clarity, absolute precision: a patch of clean in the grainy, clinging breath from the marsh that somehow, some way, would always creep into the house.

In the warmth of the Volvo and the fading light, he fell asleep. He dreamed instantly and with clarity of Mary Talbot, but a Mary Talbot left stranded in North Street, discovered by no one but the flies. Her dark hair was blue-bottle black and seething, her flesh a plantation of both known and fabulous crawling things. Baffling to the eye, these changed and meta-morphosed with great speed. Louse became maggot became eel became... *mantis*? Scale, carapace and burnished section of something half-recognised reared up and burst into a thousand succulent, carmine worms... and she was not alone with her attendants. *He* was there with her. When he looked down to the soiled carpet there were his own shoes, slipped into that morning as he sat summoning the effort to rise.

And around them was the water rising, seeping in through the stitching, the lace-holes and the pierced pattern in the leather toes.

Hiatus

What do *I* do?

Adult Education. I educate adults – it helps them back into the 'jobs market'. This suggests that jobs – these dire, immaterial things – are something you can own, can trade in.

They say it's the new religion, Work. In the long days of the newly-introduced extended terms – when what I do stretches until sleep and only the short drive home has interrupted it – I think *they* might be right. It took Christianity – was it four, five centuries to sweep the Western World? To become the defining mind-set of everyone you knew, of everyone you could ever envisage knowing; to arrive *and stick* as the creed of choice or compulsion, so that each action was in relationship to it, the most casual assessment must take account of it?

Work did it in less than half that.

I know people have always had plenty to do, plenty of ways to keep busy – not much sitting around in the Middle

Ages, wondering what'd get you first, the boredom or the Black Death. No, I'm aware they had it rough in the past, what with having to grow their own food, getting it all in, bent double, having it appropriated by any passing band of low-lifes on horseback, growing a fresh lot. And at the end of another eighteen-hour shift, there you are on your straw pallet (whatever a pallet is, exactly) racked with insomnia. You are wondering if either or both will make it through winter: the skinniest of your pock-marked brood of children – or the cow.

These people *laboured*. But when I say Work, what I mean is proper formal employment: a position, a profession, a career. Without it, you're nobody. And I'm a believer in the new religion – or I must have been at one time. I'm a priestess in the Ecumenical Seventh Day Opening Church of Work.

Seeking initiation, the sisters come to me as novices.

I saw one of them the other afternoon. I get out in the middle of the day whenever I'm able and I caught just a glimpse of an 'ex' from across the street.

Unexpected... unlucky, right in the middle of Dial Green and three miles from my desk: *Valerie*. There was the pepper-and-salt hair, with a touch more salinity than I remembered, the same dark, woollen-mixture coat. There were also on display her familiar range of quick, nervous movements – even more pronounced to my eyes because I knew what had instigated them. She paused in front of *Jeni's Cards and Gifts*, as though actually considering one of the crude pottery figures – or maybe it would be a print of ponies galloping along a bilious yellow beach...? But as always with Valerie the hiatus was momentary. Before I could call out (if I'd been about to call

200

out, which I mightn't have done anyway) she disappeared beyond the jutting frontage of Londis.

The jumbled geometry of its heaped ingredients and special offers shielded me from view.

I scuttled away in the direction of The Square.

I chose the indirect route through Cooper's Court, just for the pleasure to my fingers of passing the much decorated *Plas Neifion* (it means Neptune Hall) and it had the bonus of putting distance between Valerie and me. Slowing rather than stopping, I touched up the oak corbels in the shape of butch mermen that supported the upper storey of what was now a long, leaning town house. I pressed my palm to the massive, ornate door-case, where sea-monsters, each with an original and wonderfully fierce expression, bore up the lintel. Conches and star-fish threaded asymmetric columns on either side. Every section of timber on show had been intricately and pointlessly decorated. The familiar impulse came over me to rouse whoever owned the place with a couple of sharp raps of the dolphin door-knocker and demand to be told why and by whom. How did this nautically-themed, mystery of a building end up here, sandwiched between a row of brick-makers' cottages and a barber's shop – and in a Welsh border village fifty miles inland?

The barber, I noticed, had a queue of near-hairless elderly men spilling out of it. Once past them, it offered yet greater security from Valerie. I thought.

Pushing through the Friday lunch-time crowd, I replayed in my head the pleasantries we *might've* exchanged – always so much less draining than having to bother for real.

Hello Ellen!

Hello Valerie, how are you?

201

She'd be flattered I could still conjure up her name after more than a year.

So many students you must've seen coming and going – but we remember you. What a difference the course made! Is it still running? Good. It changed my life. I tell everybody that. Me? Oh, yes, just mornings, so far but they've promised full-time when I've finished training – absolutely love it! A really friendly team. Dial Hill Residential Unit. Do you know it? Pop in any time you're passing – if you ever want – come and see me. I'll make sure – well, just loved the course!

The course – they all 'just loved the course'. Women Into The Workplace it's called.

Valerie would be right to be pleased – if I'd spoken her name... which I hadn't. Most of them, I just can't place afterwards. I see ninety to a hundred between September and the following July, a self-replenishing stream of hopeful vestals. They come in two varieties: young, defiant, single (first day opener: 'The Social said I'd be gettin' me bus fare *and* a meal allowance and now it's come through and there's not even enough for a week's Super-Saver ticket') and the older I-really-feel-quite-useless mums. When asked why this sudden urge to seek employment they say something along the lines of: 'Caitlin, our youngest has gone to Sheffield Hallam this year to do... um... Accountancy, Classical Greek and... something else. Of course Malcolm keeps threatening to take early retirement but he never will.'

They don't mix. They form girl-gangs. They split at coffee break. On one side it's nose-studs and 'great little dresses and tops, that Indian stall, back of the market', the other it's all matched, leather accessories supplied by Browns of Chester. From this set you overhear, 'we had it at that new Mexican place, out at Dial Green – well you can always park. Massive portions but you have to book.'

The younger ones are best. Snotty to start: 'You don't know the half of it,' they tell me, 'cushy number you've got here.' It's a point of view – but after a while they say, 'I don't know why you stick it, Ellen.' Often, Keith, my boss has just left the room – and 'Debt,' I explain. They like that.

At the end of term we release the lot of them onto unsuspecting local businesses – shops, offices, hotels. By then they're able to turn on a computer, punctuate a short sentence – and refrain from expletives as an instant recourse for dealing with the irate customer. They have been empowered.

Valerie was different though. Forty-five, well-educated, attractive if you gave points for perfect symmetry, high cheek-bones, good lip-line and teeth – although there was something old-fashioned in the way all these fitted together. Hers were features that wouldn't have looked out of place in one of those black-and-white thrillers you find yourself watching on an afternoon of uncertified sick. But Valerie would never have been cast as the home-wrecker or the nightclub singer... more the hero's dependable sister or policeman's wife. In real life she was a quick learner and pleasant enough but – and it took you only a couple of minutes to come up against this but – no one, neither tutor nor student, could stand her.

It was her jumpiness.

It was an absolute, nerve-twitching pain. While she listened to you in class, one hand flew up to her pink face, to her mousy hair, to the side of her thin neck... it did them all and began again. When she spoke one leg would be tightly crossed over the other and the suspended foot performing circles under the desk with the point of the toe. Round and round it went, faster and faster in her agitation. Mesmerizing. I defy anyone to keep half a mind on what she was saying with that party trick in progress. The woman could jitter for Britain. I suspect it wore down anyone who had to spend time in her company – what were the odds that husband and step-daughter she mentioned had been *all for* the term she was to spend with us? After the first week I found it too tempting to ignore Valerie's tense, eager gaze when asking a question… and if I looked in at the refectory, there she'd be, misfiled amidst the styrofoam cups and cling-filmed Budget Bagettes of the Day – eating alone. But she passed her course exam (such as it was) at the top of the class and came for her final interview proudly clutching the decal-edged document that certified that Valerie Wynn had successfully completed Women Into The Workplace at The Mount Community Training. (Embossed motto: *Our present to you is the future*. You couldn't make it up, could you?)

'Congratulations,' I said for the tenth time that morning. The single, paper-streamer of a word fluttered to the floor like a soiled, much-trodden-on flier. 'Now what? D'you have any interviews coming up? Any help I can give with preparation or….'

'I haven't really looked yet.'

'Oh? I can get on to the job centre right now. You've done really well. There'll be no problem with a reference. To be honest, with some of the students you really have to scrape around to find something positive to say, but with you…'

In my unease I was becoming indiscrete, but it hardly mattered. She cut me off.

'I might look for something with social services.' She smoothed an imaginary crease from her well-ironed skirt with red fingers that looked as though they had been scrubbed rather than manicured. 'I feel I'd like to work with children now. Care assistant, perhaps.'

'You can do better than that.'

'I didn't think I could do anything until... here.' Her restless, pale eyes caught mine for a single heart beat before skittering away. 'You see, I've never been able to work... not since... all these years... not since....'

My empty stomach tensed.

Oh no. Not now. I've got six more to do and my lunch hour's already down to thirty minutes and I'll never get to the bank.

But, 'Not since?' I asked.

'I killed someone,' Valerie said.

Beyond my closed door the constant tramping feet failed to pause at Valerie's confession. Groups, seminars and practical sessions stop and start now at times dictated by sponsoring bodies, room availability or heating failure. They're staggered. It's never quiet.

'*What?*'

'I was a probationer – it was twenty years ago, at least. I was still just a probationer – that's a nurse, I mean. You wore a special hat in those days, while you were... always my dream to go into nursing. I went down to London to train. Paddington. I hated it, actually – I only knew round here. It was just so different down there and I didn't make many... it was all very... it was all very, um... Mrs Thatcher, you know?'

'O-kay.'

'But, stick it out, I thought, get through it. Once you're qualified you can go anywhere. And I did stick it out. I was nearly up to Christmas and I had to work over Christmas but

205

the New Year they were giving me off. I was coming home if I could manage not to catch the flu. Lots of people – staff, I mean – were off with the flu and the wards were full.'

The natural intensity with which Valerie did everything almost had me convinced I could hear the coughing from inflamed lungs, sniff the carbolic. Outside, beyond the levelling effects of sickness on the wards, there'd be a whole threatening city of power-dressing high-achievers, women with sharpened heels, wide shoulders and male incomes: bandit country to the likes of Valerie. And me.

'Anyway,' now the voice dropped to the volume of the confessional, 'there was this old man on Men's Orthopaedic. He'd been brought in after a fall, but then he developed a chest infection and he lived alone and so – well, he had to... stay on, even though we'd set his arm.'

'Right.'

'And one afternoon – it was Christmas Eve, actually – he didn't look too good. His breathing, you know? – so I went and told Sister – there was just me and her because Staff Nurse was on her break....'

Valerie's breathing didn't look too good either, in my untrained estimation. Hyperventilation – you needn't be wearing a special hat to see that. I thought: she'll become light-headed – worse, keel over. And there I'll be, closeted with an unconscious, middle-aged woman, all slack, raw hands, splayed legs and rumpled, unfashionable clothes: an inconvenient responsibility... an embarrassment... and *pathetic*. 'You don't have to tell me this, really, if you'd rather not. It sounds very personal...'

'I've never told anyone about it, before. Never!' The bright plastic chair creaked as the wretched figure, arms wrapping the body for comfort, rocked herself back and forth. 'Sister

206

brought the doctor – only very young he was, not much older than I was then – and they moved the old man... um, Albert. His name was Albert Hoskins. They moved Albert into a better position and tried to wake him... but he didn't respond. Though he coughed – which is usually good, you want them to do that to clear – but it was pink and that wasn't good. You could see it, all down his pyjamas.' Valerie could see it and round and round went the toe of her shoe, rewinding the years. 'So – they carried on... you know, with him and they sent me for the oxygen kit. It was kept – anyway, I couldn't get into the store and then I got Staff Nurse to open up and... I had trouble getting it through... we had these double doors that I couldn't get to stay open...' Her hands flicked across the emptiness between us as those troublesome doors closed, yet again, in her face. 'And when I got back – when I finally got there, he was dead. Albert had... just... died.'

'Oh... yes... but look...'

'He was just lying there – with his mouth still open. For a moment I thought it was surprise at having died – you know, like that, with the tea just about to be brought round and Staff Nurse on her break. But then I realised I was being stupid. He was just... trying... to breathe. The doctor looked at his watch and started writing up the chart – and Sister said to me, 'You took your time.' And then nobody spoke. And they never said anything about – you know, not afterwards. Nothing. Not even when I left. Which I did – because...'

That foot was stilled, mid circle.

'We'd lost other patients. It wasn't because Albert died – or not so much. It was me not... not... not being able to...'

'But you didn't kill him,' I said. 'I'm sure she, Sister, didn't mean anything like that. *You* didn't kill him.'

207

Valerie risked a series of quick glances at the ludicrously embossed declaration of merit as it lay on the desk. Perhaps to make sure it was really for her. *Valerie Wynn: Information Technology 89%, English & Communications 72%, Maths 88%, Organizational Skills 94%, Timekeeping and Attendance – Excellent.* 'Anyway,' she said, 'thanks for – well, for all your help. If nothing else, you've made me believe I can do... something. I might go and work for my husband – in the shop, you know?' I didn't. 'If the idea with the children doesn't come off. Yes. Thanks, Ellen.'

'No problem. It's what I'm paid for. But look, it seems to me you need to talk to someone about this. If it's still bothering you. I know it was a long time ago but it looks to me like it's still bothering you.'

Suddenly she was standing up. 'No. Really. Thanks. I think things are going to be... better now. Yes, I do. Thanks.'

The door slammed before I could get one more word out. If I'd had a word. A good enough word.

For me and my brain, not a lot of just-sitting-and-thinking goes on most weekdays, but we did some then, about Valerie: all those details I'd made sure not to notice about Valerie – and the snippets that she'd let slip – crowded in. There'd been the one about her step-daughter I recalled: 'Phoebe – *me* give advice to Phoebe? Oh, I don't think so.' How she'd laughed, genuinely laughed for the only time.

And for my part, there were the clangers.

Of course you're allowed to defend yourself, Julie, but for every customer you kill, that's a lost order. Reasonable force, remember.

Come on Pam! Whoever's waiting for that invoice will've died by now. You'll have to sue the estate.

Not to mention: *The Health and Safety Executive must be informed of every fatality at work*.

Straight at Valerie.

You took your time, Valerie.

She forgot her certificate. I had to post it on.

I was at a table in the window of The Square Patisserie, watching heavy traffic inch through the ancient market place. Just opposite where I was seated, a huge battle-scarred old tree (strictly speaking the property of the dental clinic) jutted into a tributary-thoroughfare barely wider than a country lane. The tree was a lime. It was in full, untidy, heart-shaped leaf: great thick suckering masses of foliage which further constricted the carriageway. So when a Parcel Force van met a scowling family in a Ford people carrier, the system threatened to crash. Horns blared, heads turned. Neither professional driver nor proud father would pause in his thrilling ten-mile-an-hour progress. I waited for the crumpling-can-broken-bottle-noise so particular to vehicle impacts... which never came. The van gouged a strip of bark from the unlucky living bollard while the courier shouted obscenities. The whole of the Ford family (children included) returned them and sped on their journey. It wasn't a novelty. Only once had I seen the competitive spirit of The Square's users give way when a young girl on an absolute monster of a horse had ridden confidently into the melee.

Just like pressing a button: everything paused.

Beautiful, she was – unruffled, as though a vision out of the distant past. As though long before Dial Green grew up here and the buildings crowded in and the streets turned impassable through usage, she'd ridden this track: as of right,

209

tranquil and alone. On the cars' roofs she looked down, not acknowledging their occupants. Bus and truck drivers she stared out. So compelling was the rider's face that I'm straight and I couldn't help but follow it with my eyes. She made them sting with yearning, though it was an objectless yen. Still, they watered away in the exhaust fumes and the prickly heat.

And it had been a while back now, and was becoming, all the time, more fantasy than genuine recall: the halted traffic, the redheaded girl perched on a shiny brown creature the height of an ambulance.

'That fuckin' tree's gonna cause a serious accident one of these days,' Carly-Jane, (*'your waitress for today'*) muttered. 'We'll 'ave 'em comin' through this glass.' Expertly she flicked someone else's crumbs into my lap, making room on the varnished but unwiped table top for my order.

I didn't say anything. I was off-duty, and more-importantly, off the premises. (The Square Patisserie may not have the ambiance of 'that Mexican place' nor its ease of parking but neither can someone – I mean Keith – demand my current student retention figures while I try to fork down the vegetarian option). Carly-Jane delivered my selection a single item at a time while the index finger of her other usable hand mined for earwax. But I was an experienced luncher here. My choice came vacuum packed by Flintshire Foods and sported a sell-by date in the next decade.

Only Robbie Williams recurring was going to get me down. 'Can't you do anything about the music?'

'Crap, huh?'

'I'd rather listen to somebody else's ringtones.'

'Boss's choice, innit?'

I just had the new Times Ed. Supp. open at FE and Private Colleges and ready to scan when, 'Hello Ellen,' that familiar voice said. *Valerie*. Of course, Valerie. I was prepared and not solely by that priming glimpse of her earlier, in the town. No – this lunchtime I'd been seduced or goaded into sifting through the vacancies, something I hadn't exerted myself to do in months. It could only be at her prompting.

Valerie (or something connected with Valerie) had long ago seeped into and dried on the cover of my mind-file labelled Work. Hers was the apocryphal tale I'd discovered the truth of, the stale coffee grounds in today's new cup. And this *despite* her being one of those lines of enquiry (I'm sure everyone has them) that I tried never to follow too closely.

Like the balance on my Visa card.

'Hello Valerie. How are you?'

The question was a mere conversational filler. It was more than obvious how she was. Bad stuff had been going on in this life – or in Valerie's case, very bad stuff... and then worse stuff. She was blinking too often – a new annoyance in her vast repertoire. And the skin across her cheekbones was blotched and coarsened as though something she was eating – *or on* – was having its revenge.

'Fine. Well, all right. Thanks. And you?' She noted, in quick succession, the sunken cappuccino froth, the half-eaten carrot cake, friable as cat-litter, the exploded sugar sachets... my choice of reading matter. 'Not leaving the college, are you?'

'It's only a training centre.... Oh well, maybe – always on the look out for something better – or at least different. How about you? Are you working?'

She was embarrassed, I could tell, and not by her dull, growing-out bob and the same old coat which, close to,

showed pulled threads, specks of lint and shed animal hairs...
and a dried white deposit of something spilled down her front
and never sponged off. Bad stuff. I remembered her as clean
and pressed to within an inch of her life.

A renewed attack of blinking came over her and died
away.

'*Whether I'm right or wrong!*' sang smug Robbie. But the
sadness behind those haunted eyes of Valerie's just kept on
being there. I saw it more clearly, now, that sadness – two
parts anguish, one of bewilderment.

She was sorry to have to disappoint. 'No,' she said.
Suddenly – *please God, not now!* – tears threatened. 'I never
did... you see, I never did get that job.'

For one awful moment it looked as though she were
considering joining me. Her hand whipped out and touched
the vacant chair... once, twice... but I had my car keys
snatched up and my money (minus tip) on the table, the
unconsidered 'exciting opportunities' scrunched together
ready for recycling. I was getting up to – no, I was on my feet.

'Got to go,' I said, brightly as I could – and truthfully.
'Back on for two.'

Weed

Becky Chapman's mother was waiting for him when he returned from burying Alf Jones... and his head was still full of Alf Jones' life as he drove up to find the determined little woman on the pavement.

'Can I have a word, Matthew?' The tone was formal, the aitch of 'have' carefully pronounced.

She had him at her mercy, trapped down here, strapped into his seat but prevented from driving onto his own property. The weak smile he managed was not returned. 'Well, yes.' Only then did she take a concessionary step backwards, hitching the strap of a multi-buckled bag further up her shoulder, business-like, impatient. Her thick hair looked newly cut and dyed into a glossy black rondure. The eyes were darkly made-up also but these were puffy and red-veined and held a wariness that undermined the hair's defiant bounce. Something – she had come for something very specific, he guessed, and yet didn't trust him to deliver it.

'I'm just back from a funeral. But I....'

He imagined her sigh at his needing two attempts to reverse the car onto the flaking surface of the drive. She tapped her foot to some inner tune as he struggled with the weird contraption that was meant to foil another unscheduled night-time outing for his meagre hatchback. 'Sorry about that, it's just that, well you have to get into the habit or the one time you forget...'

'It's about our Becky,' she began.

'Yes, yes, of course it is. Come inside.'

He led her through into the completely square front room that he kept neat for the reception of parishioners. It was furnished with a pair of small leather chesterfields (donated by his parents following their last move) and a low table with the quarterly magazine of The Royal Society For The Protection Birds and, of course, the latest Christian Aid leaflets. Apart from the framed photographs of his younger self, clasped familiarly by a surrounding group of African children in very strong sunlight, the space might have passed for the waiting room of a dentist or osteopath. 'Sit down, June,' he said and saw the words condense in three puffs of white. The room was heated only when needed and, despite the absence of cat hairs on the patterned rug or dust in the buttoned wells of the sofa arms, couldn't have been less welcoming.

'Tea or coffee?'

It had been cold and damp, lingering outside the crematorium while a few of the familiar faces in Alf Jones' vast retinue came over to give a quick critical review of his performance.

'You should've mentioned the dogs and the ponies, Mr Humphries. Loved a bet, old Alf did. Kept him going, I reckon.' This from a wheezy, old mourner/spectator that he couldn't quite place. He found his brain associated the man – somehow – with the local garage.

'Really? No one said.'

'No, they wouldn't would they? Not the close family wouldn't. Might think you'd not approve.'

'Why would I disapprove? I think it's – well, Islam, of course, has a problem with gambling. The Methodist Church won't take money from the Lottery Fund – but that's as much a social statement – concerning the general good, you see? It's far from a condemnation of individuals.'

He was encountering it more and more often, this widespread belief that all the religions had now banded together to prohibit virtually everything people were inclined or accustomed to do. Twice in the previous month (although under what circumstances he couldn't recall now) he'd been asked if he ate meat. And although, as it happened, he'd been seriously considering vegetarianism, the complexities of explanation were beginning to threaten his resolve.

'Ah, well, he'd have liked you to mention it, about the horses, old Alf would.' The speaker had shaken his head, sadly, and walked away.

'Sorry – I'm sorry, June. Did you say you wanted tea?'

June Chapman was perched now on the very edge of one sofa, her hands thrust deep in coat pockets where they squirmed and bunched as though delving still further into the garment's padding – but perhaps it was no more than the chill, the wait… as he lit the gas fire he noticed for the first time how the leather was starting to crack from its too-close position to the single source of heat. He could imagine his mother's exasperation, could foresee several futile attempts to rearrange the cramped room.

'No, nothing thanks. I'm on at the Spar, half-three. Becky's back home – came the night before last.' She swerved to her line with full-throttled monomania. 'It's a start, I guess.'

He nodded, encouragingly.

'But, of course, I *knew*. Soon as she comes back, I knew. One minute she's being one of the Dixie Chicks and we're having a laugh, next thing she's smashing the place up. Now it turns out she's having this baby.' With a local turn of phrase, the Chapman woman had managed to make it singular, a special occurrence. The indulged, wild child wasn't just pregnant. She was pregnant with *this* baby.

'Oh dear. Is there a boyfriend?'

'Well there's been one, hasn't there?' she laughed coarsely. 'She's fifteen. There's been half a dozen.' She was explaining this to him, as though at some time he'd chosen to step off the normal life-escalator and had to be told what was waiting for the rest of humankind on the store's upper floor.

'So how can I help?' He spread his hands to the fire's radiance, wished that she'd allowed his making of the tea (which he longed for).

'She'll have to get rid of it. I've told her.'

'Oh.'

On the front cover of *Birds (Autumn Number)* a huge herring gull was caught in the act of thrashing a slim, glistening eel against the rocks. He felt June Chapman inspect him with her reddened, pleading eyes. When she followed his gaze down to the tabletop she teased out one of those annoying slip-in

216

leaflets that every magazine came with, even from charities. This one was entitled *Mobile Accessories*. He felt the corners of his mouth twitch. An allusion was responsible – something someone had said to him about *mobiles*, very recently, very softly... a giggle...

'That's all right, isn't it? Getting rid of the baby? The church isn't bothered about abortion, is it?'

'Oh, you can't say that. Of course the church is concerned. I'd be concerned.'

'Yes – yes, but,' the impatience of her tapping feet had travelled straight through her. Down in the pockets again the hands were fists. Now she flicked the unnaturally blue-black hair once, twice... 'but it doesn't stop it, does it? Not like the Catholics?'

'The view taken is...' he hated himself for this beginning but couldn't find another, 'the view taken is, termination of a life – a potential life – is always a cause for sorrow – but that... that in certain circumstances it's viewed... it can be seen as the lesser of two evils.'

'That's it. Exactly. It's the lesser of the two things.'

'Evils.'

'She sits her GCSE's in six months time. All set to go to Catering College until this year – well you know.'

He knew. Her mother had wearied him, detailing the tideline trash of misery caused by Becky Chapman's hormonal surges. Nothing could halt her rampage through the village: cautioned for criminal damage, banned from The Pair of Pigeons long before legally she were able to enter it. An encounter with her one night had puzzled and then depressed him: she'd been centre stage in a group of raucous girls who screamed and jostled each other with the sort of rough, play-violence once only boys used. He hadn't spoken. One of them – Becky perhaps – had shouted 'Cocksucker!' to his back.

But the next week (bottle-green uniformed, rucksack askew), 'Hiya Matthew,' she'd greeted him.

'She says she won't get rid of it... because God'll punish her. Can you credit it? I don't think she even believes in God. It's just an excuse to get out of school.'

His outstretched leg was becoming uncomfortably hot but he rubbed it rather than move out of the fire's radiance. Easy to see what the sofa was having to endure.

'Will you talk to her? She won't listen to me.'

'I'll be pleased to see Becky, you know that. But I can't talk her into having an abortion. That'd be wrong.'

'But the church says it's all right.'

'I mean it'd be wrong for me to persuade her. I think it'd be wrong for anyone to persuade her.'

'Well, that isn't what I meant!' June Chapman's tone was suddenly suffused with open anger. It began deep in her tensed neck, swept across her face in a flush, became brilliant ruby in the marked-out channels of her eyes. He understood; the fragile model of a future she'd constructed so carefully, so painstakingly, over a sleepless night was missing a single piece. Not a very significant piece, as she saw it, and one somebody else had in stock. 'I just want...'

'Bring her round. This evening, if you like.'

'I suppose,' she allowed and in mumbling her lower lip transferred the ochreous pigment (a colour he couldn't help flinch from) to her upper teeth. Suddenly the whole rationale for the meeting seemed to have shifted. It was at his instigation... he was the supplicant.

'I don't know,' she said. 'I mean – she's difficult, you

know? She might not come, not with me. I'll try and get her –
but it might be tomorrow – depends what mood she's in. I
can't promise a time.'

The longed-for tea cooled on the mantelpiece. It had been
delayed by the arrival of his verger, Fred Gwilt, who now
occupied June Chapman's seat on the chesterfield.

He was especially anxious to cut this interview short. Fred
smelled strongly of stale urine and the precious heat of the
room would now have to be lost to ventilation the instant he
could be got rid of. But no, on he chuntered about some sort of
plant that was invading St Peter's churchyard. It was forcing its
way through the flagstones, even over-running the graves.

'It's up through two of the Prossers. Split the old
inscription right across, the one about "Captain Kenyon
Prosser was wounded at the Battle of Mons". Terrible to see
that. And all those Davies's in the far corner are sprouting
now, by the tap.'

Lacking social interactions, much of Fred's time was
spent conspiring with and cosseting past parishioners – a huge
mob of folk in comparison to the present few. There was
genuine indignation in the set of the verger's heavy jaw for
the disturbance of his charges. Fred, Matthew realised, saw
himself as a night porter in an establishment where the guests
were due an undisturbed rest.

'Oh, yes... by the...' That tea would be completely
undrinkable now. 'Tap. The Tap Davies's.'

Fred stared.

'Can you not just – oh, I don't know – pull it up, Fred?'

Fred sneered; the grey stubble of his upper lip stretched
to a smudge revealing a pair of brown rat's incisors. (Would

Jesus, he demanded of himself, notice or care about such things? Would our Lord's nose be twitching at the wave of ammonia breaking through the room at the visitor's every movement?) 'Pull it up? Only makes matters worse pulling it up.' His agitation bathed Matthew in a double dose of bitter vapours. 'You know the thing I mean, do you?'

'Knotweed, you said...'

'*Japanese* knotweed! Different thing entirely. Haven't you never heard of it? It's a *scourge*, that's what it is.'

'Oh, is it?'

'It's taking over whole – whole places!'

'Well, obviously we shouldn't let that happen.'

'But how you going stop it? Eh? How you going to get rid of something like that?'

June Chapman, all over again, he saw. Perhaps that was his function, to shoulder other people's problems, to let them walk away free and clear. *He* had desired the fecund Becky be brought before him for a good talking to. Not content with this display of spiritual grandeur, here he was at it again, requiring that his good old verger cleanse church ground of some green asylum-seeker.

'So what shall we do, Fred? It's not as if the graves in that area are well-tended, is it?' This was a euphemism for plainly abandoned – in fact, if he could visualise the Prosser graves accurately, all that was left of them was that single, poignant headstone, sticking up through the couch grass at a rakish angle. The last Prosser had left the area some years ago at the time of the foot-and-mouth epidemic – and by the state of the family plot, they were never a sentimental clan.

Ironic that the poorer offshoot of Prossers lay undisturbed beside a mean, brick chapel up on the hillside. No knotweed up there, teasing with rooty fingers the plate from the coffin-lid, the flesh from the bone. A shiver ran through him that was not of post-crematorium chill entirely. He thought: The diminishing of The Church of England in Wales could be no more neatly expressed – it failed to provide comfort even for its deceased communicants.

'Why don't you try strimming this stuff, just to keep it from spreading? What does it look like, by the way?'

Fred's grin was huge, revealing not just the teeth but the black vacancies beyond. 'Yes, you see that's what somebody who knows nothing about it might think. Just cut it down. Hack it off. Worst thing you could do!'

'I wasn't going to do it.'

'What we need is chemicals. Strongest stuff there is.'

'Really? I suppose, if it's going to be a pest then we'll have to do something – I'm not *keen* because the children play in there and then people walk through with their dogs.'

'Shouldn't be there though, should they?'

'Dogs? No they shouldn't – I suppose. I mention it now and again, in the notices. There was a time, though, when animals were sort of tolerated. I went to Shotwick church – St Michael's, on the Wirral? – last summer. They've still got the old box pews, the idea being you shut the door to keep out the hounds and any other passing mutts. Which suggests to me they'd have been whizzing round the body of the church while the service was going on! Imagine it.'

'I can't stand dogs,' Fred told him, 'and if you ask me, a lot of these kids are worse. Filthy, the stuff they leave round the graves. Filthy little...'

'All right,' he thought he might spare himself Fred Gwilt's take on the personal hygiene of others. He stood up. 'Can you find out what you think you need – what you think might do the job, in this case – and let me have an idea of cost?' He took a deep breath, meaning to hold it as long as he could. Who knows, it might last him long enough to see his guest out?

It could have worked, had Fred not stalled just on the spot where to open the front door would mean dealing the verger a blow to his left side. Still, it was tempting. 'Don't worry 'bout the cost,' Fred counselled. 'Weed killers – load of rubbish the stuff they sell now. Chemicals is what's going to do it. I'll get George to give me something off the farm. George Davies – it's his Enid's grave's being overrun. One of the worst. Only been in a year...'

'*No!*' What he meant was he needed no reminder of George's late wife. 'You see, I don't want everything...' *dead* almost slipped out but he substituted *brown and shrivelled* in time. 'We'll have a look at it tomorrow. Bye Fred.'

A quick scan across toward the church and down into the village revealed no sign of Becky Chapman's drag-footed approach. This was good. He slammed the door just, he suspected, as Fred was turning to deliver one more horticultural put-down. Even better.

The room had been fully aired, he hoped, and was on the way to being re-heated by the time his expectant ears caught Bron's key in the lock. He hurried out to meet her in the hall. She was already unzipping her jacket, of course, everything she did being quick and decisive, and with the other hand snapping shut the door. When she turned he saw her cheeks flushed with the raw, dying day outside. 'What can you smell?' he demanded as he took her by the shoulders and pulled her to him and squeezed.

'Er-m – that was nice. There's keen! Just give me a second,' she swept off the bright blue scarf in a single, graceful arc of a movement but in wriggling out of the coat, let her rush carrier of shopping drop to the floor. A bottle clinked against some other item, a tiny mobile phone slid out and she caught his eye. Very deliberately, she turned it off.

'Right – what can I smell? I can smel-ll... Fred Gwilt!'

'Bugger!'

'I know. Germ warfare's got nothing on our Fred. What did he want?'

'Germ warfare – that's spooky. It's something growing in the churchyard he wants to kill. Knotweed. Not just any old knotweed. This is *Japanese* Knotweed. Very bad, apparently. Upsetting the interred.'

'Very thick with the ex-locals is our Fred.'

The peck she gave him was so brief he hardly registered it as a kiss at all, just as contact with her chilled lips. She hurried past and made for the fire. 'Where did Fred sit?' When he indicated, she took the other sofa, throwing herself back in it so that her long trouser-clad legs stretched out to the fire and her toes, from which she allowed her shoes to slip, were no more that a few inches from the glowing flames. She held up one foot, experimentally, to see if she could touch the chrome grille with a pointed toe. 'When I was little my gran always said that's how you got chilblains – you know, you come in with frozen hands or feet and you really want to warm them, but if you do, something worse gets you.'

'Typical.'

He thought she looked beautiful, a long slim line of a woman – very much a woman despite the asexual charcoal trousers and the boyish shortness of her grey/blond hair. 'He's right, Fred I mean, about the knotweed. It's getting onto the river bank by the bridge. The thing's spreading everywhere. Not that *you'd* notice. Long stems, heart-shaped leaves? Course not! Why someone'd bring it into the country – it makes no sense. It grows like mad. It's all around the pub car-park.'

'Perhaps it'll cover up the litter. And that pile of rubble Mac's dumped.'

'There are white flowers in the summer but you need glasses to see them. I bet *you* wouldn't know it if I put it in the salad.'

'Come here.' He had squeezed in beside her.

'That's the problem with this generation gap thing. You're interested in gardening, he's sex-mad.'

'Gardening – *you*?'

'I used to cut the lawn – when we had the house.'

'Miss it, Mrs Spicer?'

'I don't miss the co-owner of the lawn, if that's what you're after.'

The few words were a catalyst; a surge of wanting, of acquisitiveness sent one arm around her back, the other up under first one layer then another of material until he found the flesh of her left breast. 'At least you're warm in there,' he muttered to the side of her neck. The nipple under his palm reacted. While they kissed, she managed to slide down (it was easy on the smooth leather) and beneath him. With him half on the floor and half on top of her most of their bodies came together.

'My toes are roasting,' she whispered as she broke free.

'We'll go upstairs.'

'Too cold.'

'I put the radiator on before you came in.'

'Now there's romantic.'

When he turned away from her and sat down he saw it had gone dark; only the dancing gas-jets illuminated one cheekbone, the side of her nose, her eyes. The firelight had made a girl of her. 'You're lovely.'

'Aren't I? Go on then, get up there and start warming the sheets. I've got something– in my bag.'

'Don't leave any lights on down here, then it'll look...'

'I know. You want the fire off?'

'Waste not, want not.'

As he ran up the stairs he felt a momentary twinge: Becky Chapman. But it was nowhere near as strong as the jolt, the quickening of energy that had hit him while down there next to Bron. This was coiled for the present in the pit of his stomach, a jack-in-a-box. But the spring – dear Lord – the strength of that spring. He had to stop himself from shouting aloud as he took the treads two by two and once in the bed his bare skin could anticipate the feel of her, the jut of hip-bones, the almost-flat soft droop of the breasts – she was a woman who'd born a couple of children nearly twenty years ago – and the live fawn nipples... she had her hand on him before she was fully in beside him: her never speaking and hardly uttering a single sound during sex was something he'd grown used to. He pulled her over and on top of him and kept her there. It was up to her: immensely important that it was up to her when he entered, how rapidly he entered, how long he stayed. Gently and languorously she settled and circled him with her burning self. Her eyes were closed and whatever went on behind her eyes was all darkness to him – and he knew better now than to try to touch her face or stomach, hold her by the hips. Only when she relaxed forward onto his chest did

225

he let go – he had no need to thrust, just let go. Breathe in and the animal scent of their combining filled his lungs, out and it was over.

Oh, God.

Seriously, what were You thinking of?

A gift can be given in many ways. With love, with mischief... was it mere curiosity? Just to see how we'd handle a morsel of power, we men?

She walked around the bed naked and came and hunkered down by the one lamp on his side. How the taking off of her clothes could strip away the years – amazing that, despite child-bearing, her body owned to so much less than her face. Her nipples were black and puckered, now, in the half-light, the darkest features since she bleached her pubic hair to platinum. Every long muscle and tendon in her body strained to maintain the balance of the crouch and their tensing showed beneath the cream suede of her skin; suddenly she was ageless, sexless – she was inhuman, she was a swan, the companion of blessed Hugh of Avalon, pure and unreachable... she was a seraph and the sphere of illumination in which she was poised flowed from within her, was made by her to fall on the crescent of bedcover, his own arm at rest on it and the lamp itself....

'You OK?' He nodded. The phosphorescent moment that had flared went out.

With her beautifully slim hands, with her painted nails, she rolled them a joint and her finger ends became translucent as they flickered in the task before the bulb. The first drag he coughed out; she took it from him – *Waste not want not!* – and stretched back beside him under the covers, dreamy and silent. He reached for his watch.

A while later she asked, 'Matthew?'

'Yes?'

'What's the time?'

'Six – gone six by now. Are you on tonight?' One of her several jobs was behind the bar at The Pigeons.

'Nah – told Mac he could do without me.'

Six gone six. He rolled it around in his head. *Lucky six. Gone six.* They must've missed the sweet chimes of the wall clock down in the hall but his mind, a roving spy, glanced off the carved walnut case, pricked itself with the arrows of the hands and skittered down the hall to the kitchen. A tap dripped out the seconds here into the sink. The fridge intoned its collect to cold and on the gas boiler top a frail old cat, a recent stray, snoozed through the hours. And it was all ravishing: the leaves and rowan berries and stems plucked up out of the walnut grain by an anonymous craftsman a hundred years ago, and growing deeper and richer and smoother with each one of them that passed... and the crystal explosions of water droplets that lay in the sink, adding to themselves or remaining discrete, sacklets of water that mocked liquidity... and the cat. The separate colours of its tortoiseshell fur rippled apart and recombined with its breathing. In a feline dream the paw reached out, dabbed... relaxed; the sorrel curve of it across the white enamel was as precisely apt as the woodcarver's scrollwork – and *live*.

It gave him a sense of deep, dizzying joy.

Another long period of quiet came next, in which he felt himself lift gradually from the bed, from his own body, and hover just below the grey of the ceiling. He came to rest able to take in the entire room below (although there'd been no sensation of revolving, which his mind told him would be absolutely essential for this to be taking place). Interesting. With sufficient concentration movement might even be possible *across* the room. And it was: now over towards the curtained window, now back again, using the beacon of the lamp... this was what it meant to be the kestrel he'd seen this morning. High up on the shoulder of Moel Ferch, it had loitered, pinned against the sky and leaning on a nothingness that must've felt solid and dependable to the bird. *Look down*, it had goaded him – *nothing to fear*.

'I love you Bron,' he thought he said. There Bron lay quiescent, in the attitude of a pale corpse, the bright end of the joint like a magic ring, glowing with its own energy... and then there was his own hand, taking it from her, kindling it to extra brightness at his mouth.

This time he drew the smoke in more deeply; it stayed.

'I love you Bron,' he exhaled.

Somewhere there was a knock on a door – not the response he was expecting. He conjured in a leisurely way with the possibilities – which door? Whose knock? Nobody answered, of course. For himself, it would have been beyond impossible. He stared hard at Bron, wondering if by effort of will he could get her to go in his stead – but she, absolute in passivity, was making it clear she wouldn't be stirring.

A second, less gentle tap and – His patience having worn out – God walked in.

The recognition was instant although God was much shorter than he'd been imagining for all these years – and very *casual*. Having coughed politely, and cleverly avoiding the trip-hazard from the trailing flex, He came and sat down at the end of the bed. He could be a family member, a hospital visitor, someone expected and....

Ah-h! Very light, was God. Insubstantial as the kestrel, He must be. There was no depression in the covers, no sound from a bedstead that accompanied the lover's every move with tuts and grunts. Many of God's facial features, he noted, seemed to be shared with that old man always found hanging around the garage: deep hollows where the cheeks had fallen in over lost teeth, some sort of hairy cyst or growth between the brows. But God's overalls were snowy white.

His and God's eyes locked.

Are You watching me always?

Bron's small noises told him she was asleep and would not interrupt this tete a tete. But her heat flowed through him like a benediction and with each nasal breath (she had a virus coming on by the sound of it) he was soothed and emboldened.

Was it a flicker of the lamp – or did God blink?

Are You – forgive the question even as it forms now, Sir – are You jealous?

Acknowledgements

Thanks to Peter Johnson and John Dixon – both history men – for their help with 'Morfa' and especial thanks to my editor Gwen Davies: sharp but never cutting.

'Residue' and 'Living in Hope' both appeared in *New Welsh Review*. 'Dinner on the Roof', 'Treeline' and 'Auntie Shar's Seasoning' were broadcast by BBC Radio 4 and produced by Jane Dauncey and Alison Hindell. 'All The Rest' was first published in *Real Writers*.

G